# Hangnails

## DEVON ASARO

# DEDICATION

Cory Monteith

# CONTENTS

# ACKNOWLEDGMENTS

Page, Susan, Jessica, Craig, Pam, Donna, Debbie, Candace, Van and David.

# PART 1

# 1. MEAN STREETS

Tuesday morning, I am feeling a little less heartbroken than usual when I arrive at my acting school. But my hatred for Beth has grown. I had picked out an outfit, checked that it didn't look horrible before I walked out the door, even did my hair and makeup.

Okay, so I did a spectacular job on my hair, makeup and outfit. It took me an hour and thirty minutes to get ready. Yet the look isn't for me or a guy. It is a sad and pathetic way, the only way I can think of to better myself in front of Beth.

I have class with her on Tuesdays. I didn't always hate her. My hate used to be only a moderate dislike, but since Matt broke up with me to be with Beth, the moderate dislike became total hatred.

My past dislike was because Beth's daddy was some quote-famous-unquote director. Beth is rich, and always missing class 'cause the hot shot agent her daddy set her up with is always calling her with auditions. Even if she didn't have a fucking famous parent, I still can't stand her ever-present East-Coast-prep-school-like tailored outfits, as if she has just stepped out of a fucking Burberry catalogue, or for her less-than-casual approach to the craft of acting.

Her overall carefree sunny attitude and togetherness makes me want to puke. She is always texting on her fancy freaking cell phone, as if she has two hundred best friends who will drop dead if they can't get ahold of Her Highness for five minutes. Plus, I automatically dislike anyone from New York.

To compensate, I behave super extra friendly, peppy and complimentary every time I talk to Beth. By mimicking her cheery bright attitude whenever she is around, I secretly hope no one will notice my Tuesday transformation, inside and out.

At first, I thought Matt was the best actor in school. Later I thought he was the laziest person ever to have lived and couldn't act if someone held a gun to his head. I hate him. He is such a coward and a pussy. When I asked him why he left me, he gave me a bunch of abstract generic bullshit answers like, "Blake, I didn't want to hurt you, you're a good person," or, "It wasn't there." Why couldn't he just have the balls to tell the truth? "After I realized you wouldn't fuck me, I didn't want to waste my time with you."

I still would have been devastated. Hated, despised and disgusted by him but would have had the slightest bit of respect for him and a straight answer, for Christ's sake. Not to mention the truth. The day Matt said we were over. I can't say the day he broke up with me because, according to him, we were never "official." I realized he flirted with everyone and kissed everyone's ass. Maybe because he knows he can't get anything with his lack of real talent or work ethic. Wouldn't know hard work if it walked up to him and slapped him across the face. He is greasy and struts around as if he is the hottest shit ever to walk the earth. But, I still wish I had some of his over-the-top misguided arrogance instead of my plummeting self-esteem. I am glad I shifted to anger when it came to Matt, versus hurt and heartbreak. But still, sometimes I think there is something seriously wrong with me for caring about and being so attracted to such a piece of shit.

Beth, Matt and I all go to The Lee Strasberg Theater and Film Institute, an acting school started by the late legendary genius of the same name. The school teaches Method Acting. That is the name of Lee Strasberg's technique. If you know anything about acting, it's the only kind of acting, otherwise you're not acting.

The school is in Los Angeles, specifically West Hollywood, in a two-story building on Santa Monica Boulevard. I have almost all of my classes with Rourke, the best but scariest teacher here.

Then I see Beth and want to die.

I am concentrating on lowering my heart rate after my first run-in with her that day when Rourke's assistant teacher George comes into my peripheral vision. I walk over to say hi to him. He is sitting at the table in the lobby with someone I've never seen before. George introduces the new guy and says, "He's special."

That *special* bugs me. What does he mean? I'm not going to ask. I am already trying hard enough to mask my insecurity. George never said *I* am special.

I internally try to calm myself down and not care. I also instantly check the new guy out; then immediately dismiss him in my mind. Apparently, Penn is his name. I never checked guys out in the past but in an attempt to do anything to get over Matt, to beat the womanizing jerk at his own lame game, to show how fucking not *good* I am, I began to.

Penn is too pretty. I don't care for pretty boys. He has blond hair, blue eyes and practically rosy pink cheeks.

Unfortunately he isn't my type, and I am sad he won't be a distraction for me so I can stop thinking about Matt.

I go to my first class of the day. The one I have with Beth. That Penn guy is in it.

Three hours and forty-seven agonizing minutes later, I am internally thanking God class is almost over with Beth when Rourke begins to assign Penn his scenes. Penn and I are assigned a scene together. Penn is given a scene with that bitch Beth, too.

Our scene is from the play *Forgotten Minds*. I have read the play before. It is about two lovers, Stacy and Dustin. They were together until Dustin left Stacy and then started dating Stacy's cousin. The scene we are doing depicts when Stacy barges into Dustin's apartment and rips him a new one right after she finds out he's been hooking up with her cousin.

## 2. BOYS DON'T CRY

One week later, Penn and I are scheduled to do our first read in front of the class. The first read represents a table read, which is what professional actors do. That's when they first meet each other before rehearsal and filming. The most important thing I need to do in the reading of *Forgotten Minds* is to begin to create the relationship Stacy has with Dustin.

I am tall with brown eyes and really long wavy brown hair that I always straighten. We stand on stage. My hair is straightened. I am wearing my tightest pair of jeans, but they have stretch to them, so I can move, and a black shirt and my caramel stiletto ankle boots with the pointy tips. But, when I get on stage, I feel too tall in them. So I take off my heels. Kind of hoping I can do the scene better without shoes. I always feel like I suck at first reads, but with Beth in the audience, I am extra-motivated to show no weakness. Therefore I prepared extra. Well I always rehearse extra, and now I am extra, extra prepared.

The read starts. Penn looks at me, and I already recognize the smirk on his face and the way he is using his eyes to flirt with me. I only think of Matt who did the same thing, but, I am supposed to be creating something with the guy in front of me. The blood starts to boil in my chest, but I am glad Penn is giving me something to work with other than a blank face. I get off to a rocky start, but after Rourke and I exchange a few words, things go relatively smoothly. Thank God, I won't have to live another day with the feeling of a scene gone terribly bad.

Penn and I get off the stage after we finish the read. We sit in front of Rourke, and he and Penn discuss what Penn did during the read. While they talk, I learn Penn is an international student from Switzerland, even though he has a perfect American accent, and that he'd spent a year at Strasberg three years ago. That he came back to brush up on his craft because there is a chance he will be cast in an independent film. He must have left right before I got here, since I have been here two years.

I don't like the history I see between Rourke and Penn. Rourke remembered that Penn has two main acting choices he uses: his girlfriend from Switzerland and his grandma who died. In acting a "choice" is someone or something emotional provoking you use to rehearse your craft and improve your talent. Rourke calls Penn "a very accomplished actor," whatever that means. So I have already added Penn to my hate list. I'm not a bad or mean person or anything. Just don't need any more competition, especially from an apparently talented pretty boy. Hollywood might buy his pretty-boy looks, but I never will. It takes a hell of a lot more than that for me to buy.

But will I, be remembered by Rourke, if I leave and come back years later? Let alone will he remember my choices?

When it is my turn to discuss the read, I tell Rourke, "I

feel self-conscious when I'm taller than my male scene partners."

He responds by reminding me that he wants me and all actors to glory in their height. I wish I didn't feel uncomfortable in my heels. I should start wearing them everywhere, every day, to rectify the situation. And, hang some sort of sign over my bed that says, "Glory in your height."

Rourke tells us to improvise the relationship for two hours, then for the last hour of the rehearsal, bring in the scene.

The intent of our improvisation, is to get things from each other we can use in the scene. Sometimes this involves provoking ourselves and each other. This shows the characters have known each other for a long time and have shared experiences. The goal is to deal with each other as real lovers do. People in a relationship have feelings toward each other so that's what we need to create. A sense of two people in a real relationship. Sometimes the acting industry calls this sense between actors "chemistry."

After class is over, I sit on the wood floor with my pile of stuff, finishing up my notes. I will always worry I am going to forget something I think of or Rourke said, so I write it all down.

Penn comes up to me and we begin talking about when to rehearse.

"I was kind of worried about the first read. I'm glad it went all right," I say.

"Maybe if I was *taller* it would have gone even better," Penn replies.

What is going on? Is he being mocking and sarcastic? It seems so. And, he even stresses the word 'taller.' I had talked about my self-consciousness of my height for a while with Rourke, but it was just business as usual, talking about the details of the scene and the work. He shouldn't take it personally or anything.

"You're probably right." I don't mean it. I just say it 'cause it is my impulse, totally different. And, to play the game because I think it might upset him.

"If I was *taller*, you might like me as a scene partner," Penn says.

He mentions taller again and uses the same inflection. I am taken aback by this. No one has stood up to me like that really, especially making some dry mockery at it. That is *my* way. He is saying it, I think, by way of asking for an apology.

I have nothing to apologize *for*. I am doing my work. I don't like that he cared and that he brought it up. Or, that he is even paying attention and that he has the intelligence to make an ironic joke. And no one else talks about or brought up the quote boring details about the work unquote. I want to be able to walk all over my scene partners or wipe the floor with them or whatever; without any personal contact off stage and out of rehearsal. Off stage and off rehearsal, everything is supposed to go on as if nothing happened, right? Maybe? Or, I don't know. *I* am the sarcastic one never wanting to get personal, even though acting is all about getting personal.

Since Matt, I never want to be hurt again. Even in the smallest way.

Penn and I agree to rehearse on Saturday. But I realize it makes me a little sad. It is only Tuesday and I won't get to spend time with him until the weekend.

The next afternoon, I see Penn again when he comes into my class. Guess we have another class together. It is Improvisation.

During the break, I sit on the bench eating a snack. And I am tired. I have pulled out a bag of cheese. I'd put it in my purse in a hurry that morning. Now it is warm. Kind of melted and deformed. Why couldn't I have thought to bring something that would hold up better? It doesn't look very appetizing, but I am hungry and there is nothing else to eat.

But it is hard to eat while that fucking boney vegan girl is staring and judging me for eating cheese. Why does she have to be sitting right next to me? Making me feel fat and guilty?

Another girl, Emily, from class is also there, talking to what sounds like her boyfriend. They discuss what they should have for dinner. I overheard a while back that they live together. Emily is complaining that she doesn't want to eat SpaghettiOs because they've had them for a week in a row. The conversation is so banal and depressing. Why can't she just shut the fuck up? That's what it will be like to live with a guy or to have a boyfriend? SpaghettiOs sound so disgusting and isn't that what five-year-olds eat?

Penn comes downstairs and starts saying that his dream is to do commercials for a living. He goes on talking about his soap days and impersonates how they talk on soaps. His body language impersonates it too; he gets all stiff. It makes me smile. He is acting like a kid, and making fun of the acting business, about how it sucks we have to do commercials and bad soap operas. I am enjoying the little show when Emily pipes up.

"Your dream is to do commercials?" she asks, with all sincerity. "Yeah, you can make a lot of money doing them."

Is this chick for real? Penn is obviously being blatantly sarcastic. He is good. He doesn't crack a smile, but the girl is too stupid to notice. Before break is over, I ask Penn to bring video of his soap opera days to rehearsal. I think it might give me something for our scene, especially if he brings video of love scenes or him kissing a girl in a clip. I want to see how he kisses and *stuff*.

After class, Penn comes over to me and calls me by my name, Blake. I'm not used to that. He goes on to say he is buying a motorcycle and asks me about the process and wonders what he needs to bring other than cash.

"What's the paperwork I'm going to get so they know I have ownership? I don't have to take a test, do I?" Penn asks.

I'm not used to people treating me like I am competent and mature; well, other than about acting. I feel flattered he asks me. He could have asked that bitch Beth, or someone else. I am turned on by the fact that he likes motorcycles, but at the same time I feel kind of weird. I immediately try to stuff the kind of weird down.

Yesterday I did an improvisation with my scene partner Jerry, and his motorcycle came up in our discussion. Rourke and I had talked about all the feelings his bike brought up and how to use them in the scene. Penn had witnessed the whole thing.

"You're asking me about buying a motorcycle? Are you doing this for the scene or is this life and you're being serious?" I ask.

Is Penn making up buying a motorcycle to work on something in the scene? To provoke me, 'cause why is he asking *me*? Or is he being real and serious and he really is buying a motorcycle and needs my advice? Was he really listening during class? Does he even remember? If this guy is apparently so fucking smart he could be using this little motorcycle lie on me. Or am I being paranoid?

"What's the difference?" He says. Long pause. "Yeah, I'm really buying one." His reply interests and intrigues me.

"I think all you need is the money. You'll get a pink slip and then set up the insurance and stuff on your own," I say still, totally confused and unsure of why he is asking me.

# 3. THE MOTORCYCLE DIARIES

On Saturday my roommate Ashley, my best friend since forever, isn't home in our two-bedroom apartment in West Hollywood.

Penn is supposed to be over soon. I am really tired. I've just gotten home from work and am hating and stressing about my job but am still thinking about the interactions between us so far and how it affects me. How I can work it into the scene.

See, I just started working part-time as a personal trainer. I've been doing it a few months, since my 21st birthday. But my anxiety rises at work. Most of my clients are female. They're 75 percent of the people who buy training. They tell me they want to lose weight and be "toned." Then when I suggest how often they should workout, five days a week usually, they don't want to do it.

I thought getting this job would help support me financially while acting, as well as educate me on how to improve my workouts because I've always been into fitness, but my clients don't listen to me. They are lazy during their own sessions and some of them don't even want their body fat percentage measured. It makes absolutely no sense to me. What should I do about them? I measure my body fat consistently. At least once every six weeks. It helps me know I am on track. When I've gone too long without knowing what number I'm at there is this haunting feeling in me, but right after I see the result, that I'm still at a low percentage, under 13 percent, I feel okay.

At this point in learning the technique of Method Acting I usually plan to fix myself up, makeup, outfit, to feel the most confident; to be able to express and follow my impulses. I think maybe it makes it a little easier. But again, my plan to get it together is falling to shit. I am so exhausted and am not even sure that Penn is going to show up. I've called him to double check if he is coming, but he didn't answer.

I change out of my work clothes. I am still so anxious, paranoid and upset about work. I hate it at the gym and just want to hide right now. I put on one of my favorite pairs of tight jeans, a black T-shirt, put my hair down and add some de-frizz stuff to it and brush on some powder. But that is all the energy I have. I put some stuff away in the apartment. I am lying on my bed looking at the scene when he knocks.

I open the door to Penn wearing jeans and a white T-shirt. He offers me a hug and I hug him back. I am surprised by his friendliness. He is acting like we already know each other. He is holding his motorcycle helmet. He comes in and the first statement out of his mouth is, "Tell me about your last boyfriend." The statement is so direct, like he has thought about it ahead of time.

"I've never had a boyfriend," I reply.

"You've never had a boyfriend?"

"Yeah, I usually lie about it but I don't feel like lying today."

I don't like that he brings up the subject of having a boyfriend. All I can think of is Matt and an achy disgust starts bubbling up. I want to not think about him every minute of the day; okay, more like every second of the day. I'm not happy that Penn starts on this topic.

"Then tell me about your last crush," he says.

I picture Matt's face. "I haven't had a crush recently."

This goes on for a while.

Later, Penn sits on my bed and I nervously pace my room.

"Why haven't you ever had a boyfriend?" Penn asks.

"I don't know I just haven't. By the way, we aren't going to be friends since you said you're only here for one semester."

Penn gets up and starts looking around. He picks up and looks at the few picture frames I have. No one else has analyzed them as much as he does. I feel nervous. I don't like how I look in the pictures and am mad at myself. I wonder why I have put them up to begin with. I grab the picture frame he is holding and put it face-down on my desk.

He keeps looking around my room. He notices my snowboard and skateboard, then looks on a shelf and points out the only candles in the room. They are leopard print.

"I bet these were given to you," he says.

Weird or maybe cool; how does he know?

"They were," I say.

"Yeah, they don't seem like you, or really go with the rest of the place, but I'm sure the person who gave them to you was very well-meaning." He is so polite and respectful even when he is trying not to be.

I continue with what I have been talking about, Ashley's ex-boyfriend. "He's a bad guy, even though everyone thought he was so great and then out of the blue he cheated on her."

"So if a guy cheats, it means he's a bad guy?"

"Yes," I say very slowly and firmly.

"Maybe it was her fault; she wasn't giving him what he needed or it was something she did."

I want to smack him across the face. I feel a sting in my chest.

"You're weird. How could you say that? She didn't do anything. Even if she did, he shouldn't have cheated. He should have talked to her or broken up with her. What's wrong with you? Why are you defending him?" I say.

He is provoking me so much. I don't know what to make of it all. At least I have someone to focus my hate on other than Matt.

After our first read, Rourke had told me to use the most personal thing I got from Penn as my "choice" for the cousin in the scene. She is the reason Stacy gets enraged. This might be it.

Later Penn tells me he has a girlfriend and that they've been together for ten years. I can't believe it, as he is so young, and ten years is such a long relationship. He goes on and lamely explains the severely fucked-up relationship between him and his true love. He says they are together but not because they've agreed to only email while he is gone.

Nothing he says makes sense, but I get the picture anyway. When he left to come to Strasberg they were sort of broken up. But when he goes back to Switzerland he will live with her again.

"When was the last time you had sex?" Penn says.

I am expecting this question by now. All my other male scene partners have asked the same thing. A typical conversation a male would bring up. I think.

"That's a rude question. When was the last time you had sex?" I ask.

"Three weeks ago, before I left."

He surprises me when he actually answers. At least he is

saying stuff. But I don't believe a word of it. I like his openness though.

He says he is going to have sex with someone else before he goes back home because he is here for three months. And three months is too long to go without sex.

I don't say anything. Just take it in and watch his face. This dysfunctional concept again reminds me of Matt's beliefs. But I don't berate Penn. I don't need to. The feeling I get will be enough. Anyway, I am playing for Matt's loser team now, so I play along.

"Well I'll call your girlfriend and tell her you said that then," I say. Then pick up his cell phone he's left on my desk, and start going through it. I am surprised he lets me. "What's her name?"

"It's in there as 'Sweetie,'" he says.

I don't like his reply. "Sweetie" doesn't seem like him. He is honest and doesn't sugar coat shit.

"I'm gonna call," I say, warning him. And play with the phone for a few minutes; then get fed up. I can't find any "Sweetie" and finally put the phone down. But keep thinking that he said "Sweetie."

"You call her Sweetie? That's lame. Did you bring your soap opera video?"

He didn't bring what I asked for, a video or reel. I am a little pissed and disappointed. But he says his phone has pictures of his girlfriend. I ask to see them. Well, when I see them they are of his girlfriend *and* him. In the pictures they are holding hands and are all fucking lovey-dovey. The girl is wearing a pink dress with tacky lace or flowers or some frilly shit on it. She has big boobs and blond hair.

"Where are all the pictures of the girls you have on the side?" I smirk.

Penn smiles. "I don't keep those pictures in there."

He plays along. I don't like that. He is supposed to defend his honor and lie and say he doesn't have any girls on the side or say, "how dare you talk like that." And say, "of course I don't have any pictures of other girls" and "I'm not like that." At least he is honest about his disgusting behavior.

"What's her name?" I ask again.

"Ella," he says.

Ella? Huh. I've always liked that name, until now.

He is looking right at me now with knowing flirty eyes or something. The same look as our first read. He's been doing this throughout the rehearsal.

"You're weird," I say.

Moments later, I say, "We have to go for a ride on your motorcycle."

Months ago, I read a script that had a bunch of guys on motorcycles racing and roaring through the desert. Ever since then I thought they were cool and exciting and was fascinated by them.

"I don't have another helmet," he says.

"That's okay. We won't go far."

"No, you need a helmet. Wait, I can call my roommate and see if she can drop one off."

"Really? Great. I've never been on one but we have to take a ride on yours."

He calls his roommate, and she agrees to drop it by. I am glad. I think I will get a good experience to use as a choice for the scene from riding on the motorcycle. Penn picks up *The Departed* movie he sees propped up on my dresser.

"That movie is so good. I love Scorsese," I say.

"I've never seen it."

"You haven't? Oh my God, it's my favorite movie."

"Mine's *On the Waterfront*," Penn says.

I pause for a second. What I know about Elia Kazan, the director of *On the Waterfront* and what any other intelligent actor would know, is that Kazan had been known for how well he could direct actors. I know Kazan started out as an actor and so would always allow them to do their work. Even though Penn has never seen *The Departed,* I forgive him because I have so much respect for his favorite movie. Not even to mention Marlon Brando plays the leading man.

Penn goes outside to fetch the helmet from his roommate, who is waiting outside in her car. Inside, I wonder what she looks like and how Penn is interacting with her. Wait, maybe I can go out and sneak a peek?

I run out the door to see if I can get a glimpse of his roommate but the chick leaves before I can see anything. All I find is Penn waving goodbye to her car. I sprint back inside before Penn can catch me and ask what the hell I am doing.

We walk outside to ride his motorcycle.

"I've never been on a motorcycle before. I'm really scared so you have to drive really careful and safe as if you were driving Elia Kazan," I say.

"I'll drive really careful."

I am trying to figure out how to fasten my helmet.

"Can I take a picture of you?" he says. He is holding up his camera phone.

"Why? Fine," I assume he is taking the picture to study it for the scene. To create the relationship between us and all that. Why didn't I think of that? I have that jealous competition feeling that maybe he has more tricks or brains up his sleeve than I do.

We get on the bike.

"I'm really scared," I say again. He remains relaxed. "Aren't you gonna tell me what to do? Should I like lean with you when you turn?"

"Yeah," Penn says.

I put my arms around his waist. "Tell me if I squeeze you too tight."

"You're fine. You can hold on tighter."

And off we go. I am worried the motorcycle will be super loud and annoying but it isn't. It is loud but a cool loud, not some souped-up shit. I am nervous I am going to get really scared and squeeze him to death from fright. I feel more than awkward about touching his waist and am concerned he can feel my bloated stomach that I don't like. We ride up to the Hollywood Hills. It is warm out but not hot. I keep waiting to get scared but I don't. Even when we go faster or when he turns and the motorcycle leans. I am having fun.

"Are you okay?" he asks.

"Yeah, I'm not scared at all."

We pull over and stop at a viewpoint. I take off my helmet, and worry how my hair looks after having it on. I wish I had a mirror. Is it really flat because of the helmet? I keep putting it up and taking it down with the black hair tie I leave on my wrist and attempt to casually and discreetly smooth the flyaways down with my hand. Hoping to not seem superficial and trying to look like one of those girls who looks absolutely perfect without trying and never gives a thought to her appearance.

As I look out over the city with Penn beside me, trying not to stress about my hair, I feel shitty. He is pointing out all the different areas of town. How does he know more places than I do? He doesn't even live here. I've hardly been anywhere in the city and it doesn't feel like home. It should have, because it is only an hour away from where I was raised.

There are other people at the rest stop. I wonder if they think anything of Penn and me. Do they think we are friends or do we look like a couple?

"I bet it would be cool to look out here at night," he says.

"What do you like better, riding at night or during the day?"

"They're different but I like things about them both. At night it's cold because I can't afford a leather jacket."

He makes me remember what a cast member in my

favorite TV show *Gold* said. "I was an actor in New York and I couldn't afford a leather jacket." In the behind-the-scenes clip, his coworkers are making fun of him 'cause he is obsessed or has a thing about leather jackets. He has a closet full of them now. I love that. Now he can buy one. He didn't forget he wanted one and remembers his shitty past. He finally got what he wanted. I just love it. I'm not exactly sure why. Maybe because it is a happy ending and he has something tangible to show for it.

As we are getting back on the bike Penn asks, "Do you want to ride longer or go back?"

"Let's ride longer."

We go through a few neighborhoods in the hills. Penn points out where he has been before. He is revisiting it three years later. He looks like he enjoys seeing parts of L.A. again and I am glad. I am getting much more comfortable holding onto him and being so close to his body. I even can relax.

We head back to my apartment, but I want to stay on the motorcycle with him for even longer. When we get back to my place Penn checks a message on his phone. I am mad he is spending time on his phone during rehearsal and think it is very unprofessional. I take my acting career seriously and every rehearsal needs to be completely focused. But when he hangs up the phone he looks sad, really sad.

"What's wrong?" I say.

He says he got a message from his sort of girlfriend, Ella.

"We were having fun and now you look like you're gonna cry," I say.

"I think she misses me."

I don't understand what it would be like to be in a ten-year-loving-complicated-messy relationship.

"Oh. I was worried we weren't going to be able to go on your motorcycle. It was nice of your roommate to drop the helmet by," I say hoping to change the subject. It is getting kind of awkward and uncomfortable.

"It was nice. We had sex one time, that was nice too," Penn says.

"Okay," I say confused.

"I'm just saying."

"Why?"

"Because it's sex," he says.

"Eww, so you just have sex with your roommate. I bet you don't even think she's pretty or respect her at all," I say feeling disgust, mad and about eighty other things.

"Yeah, it's sex," he says.

"We should probably start the scene."

We now have our scripts out, ready to do the scene. I had wanted to tell Penn he was every woman's absolute worst nightmare, and that I felt like blowing chunks, but instead said we should start the scene because I felt provoked. Just like my character did at the beginning of the scene in *Forgotten Minds*.

### Blake as Stacy:
### "How could you do this to me?"

### Penn as Dustin:
### "So I guess she told you. You look nice."

I wish I felt more comfortable with him doing the scene. Wish I could create relationship faster and wish I felt more normal acting altogether. It is still hard for me to admit to myself I want to be an actress. It seems so against the grain, but the more I act, the more I like it and the more I want it to be my life and career. Deep down in that tiny part of me that will never die or will ache if I can't act, it is there and I am beginning to trust it more.

After we get through the entire scene, Penn leaves because we have completed our three hour rehearsal time.

We say a normal "See you later" but there is an energy in the room of things left unsaid.

I turn on *The Departed* but then start to cry. I feel alone again because of all the reminders of Matt even though I made sure never to speak of him to Penn. I can't stop thinking that Penn had sex with his roommate. But he said the last time he had sex was with his girlfriend in Switzerland. And then after, said he had sex with his roommate, but that didn't make sense. Because he also said he was going to have sex with someone else meaning he hadn't done it yet. Isn't that what he said? Am I already catching him in a shitload of lies? Is he talking about the last time he was in L.A.? That they'd had sex then?

Plus I hate that Penn was not in school for very long, yet learned so much so fast. I feel slow and behind, as if I should be even further along than I am.

Tuesday morning in Rourke's class, three days later, we've just done sensory. On sensory day we do two acting exercises. One is called "relaxation" and the other is called "sensory." On this day actors work on a choice in great detail and train the capacities of the work. Which is the ability to experience and express everything going on in the script.

I am sitting in my chair, miserable, listening to Penn and Rourke discuss Penn's sensory work. Rourke asks what exercise he is working on. He says a place, specifically a lake.

I wonder if that meant he is further along in the work than I am but then I know it doesn't work that way so I try not to speculate or compare myself to him. But still, somehow I am jealous. Then Rourke says Penn even became emotional when he just said the word "lake."

Should I be like that? Or eventually be able to be like that? Why is it so provoking listening to other people talk about their work? One time, or more than one time, Rourke talked about how we should be able to create a choice or get provoked by just saying one word. Which is what well-trained actors can do. Is that really true? No, I must have misunderstood. That seems impossible. Just thinking about all this stuff is very overwhelming. Is Rourke implying that Penn knows the work well already and therefore was wondering why he had come back to Strasberg?

After all the upsetting discussion in class I rush to the bathroom. As usual, I try to dive into the work so at the end of sensory I am exhausted. An emotional wreck with fucked-up hair and makeup, which is exactly the case today. I am tired and trying to emotionally wash away what is left of the sensory exercise, which has very much included Matt.

In the bathroom mirror I am also trying to salvage what is left of my eye makeup. I am planning to look for a new job tonight after class, and I don't want my exhaustion and second-guessing of myself over how well the sensory went to stop me tonight. Or my severely pissed-off mood to stop me.

Beth waltzes into the bathroom and dabs on some lip gloss. She was calm as a cucumber the entire exercise, which probably meant she didn't know what the hell she was doing. She is in a good or even keel mood and looks all fresh and shit. I compliment her retarded leather boots, finish my own primping and leave. I want to get as far away from that bitch as quickly as possible.

I walk down the stairs into the lobby and find Penn. He isn't wearing any shoes. He has taken them off and they are lying next to him on the floor. We start to talk about scheduling rehearsal. I wish I could've looked as fresh and put-together as Beth did. Especially while talking to a boy and especially while talking to Penn.

"I have to eat dinner and digest. So maybe at 7:30," Penn says.

I love how he listened exactly to what Rourke said that day in class. I do that too, but had started to feel weird about it 'cause Matt would give me shit for it. What is so wrong with listening to my acting teacher and working hard? Rourke said that a large meal can have an impact on preparation and feeling your body sensually. You need both things to act.

Saturday night seems like the only time that will work and when I bring it up, Penn agrees.

That night I am driving home from my last class of the day. My mind drifts back to Beth as I drive and then to Beth *and* Matt. I hate them.

After I get home, I put on *The Sopranos*. I half watch and listen while I imagine Beth and Matt becoming famous and walking the fucking red carpet and me lying in the gutter. About Beth giving a superficial interview about creating the character and her time at Strasberg, and Matt talking about how much he suffered in his past and how far he has come. Everyone will call Beth beautiful and sexy, and I'll have to listen to it.

The idea makes me sick. I am hungry but can't eat and am too tired to make anything anyway. Though when I think of one imperfect thing about Beth, I notice my appetite slightly return. See, everyone does a monologue when they have their first class with Rourke. This way he can evaluate what they know about Method Acting. When Beth first did her monologue, Rourke said he could see Beth's commercial appeal. I didn't like that, although it could have been far worse. On that day or since he never once said she was even remotely talented.

Thursday, I am with Shannon, a girl from one of my acting classes. We've just been assigned a scene and I don't know her that well. We are trying to find an available classroom to rehearse.

One of the rooms we find at school is a miniature sound stage where people film short films and stuff. I hold my head and face up really close to the door to see if I can hear anyone working in there. I don't want to interrupt if people are inside. It is quiet but the door is so thick because of the soundproofing it is hard to tell.

I am at the second door inside that vestibule thing that the sound stage has when suddenly the heavy black door opens and hits me in the face before I know what is even happening. It hurts. This giant guy had pushed open the door as he was talking to his friend. He apologizes, and I say it is okay, trying not to hold a grudge even though I totally do. Does he have no spatial awareness? I begin to feel a lot of pressure build on my left eye. It stings too.

The goddamn sound stage isn't even free but eventually we find another room. Me and Shannon, who by the way has arrived late and now we have to rush, which is a very good way to screw up rehearsal to the point where it can be practically useless to do at all, finally sit down. I try to ignore my eye. I don't have time to think about it anyway since I am already in a hurry. I can't talk or explain or complain. It is time to work.

"Are you sure you're okay?" Shannon asks.

"Yeah, I'm fine," I say.

Shannon's phone beeps. She checks a text message.

"You know who Matt is, right? He says he can't rehearse later 'cause he has an audition. He's lying," Shannon says as she looks up from her phone.

"Fuck him then," I say.

"Exactly."

I exhale. "My eye hurts," I admit. Then, I take out the compact I keep in my purse. In its small mirror, I see that my left eye is a little swollen and there is a small cut with some blood.

# 4. ORDINARY PEOPLE

After work on Saturday, I plan on taking a nap before rehearsal. Or more like, I am going to *try* to nap before rehearsal because sometimes, even though I am tired, I can't sleep. It is only 3:30 p.m. but I am already exhausted. The night before, I'd been up late rehearsing and feel I can't keep up with life today, if I don't nap.

I put on my eye mask to block the light, hoping I can get quality sleep. If not, I am going to be beyond dysfunctional the entire rest of the day. I put in my earplugs, too.

I wake up glad I was able to fall asleep, but also pissed because now I am groggy and don't want to get up. I get out of bed and look at the time. I've slept longer then I wanted to. I must have hit the snooze button too many times. Now I wish I have more time to get ready.

I look in the bathroom mirror after I take off my mask and earplugs. The eye makeup I have on from work is squished all over my eyelids and under my eyes, and I have a red mark on the side of my face from the pillowcase. The small bruise on my eye has turned into a majorly swollen black eye. Before I went to sleep it was only a little black and blue but now it is twice as big and the scab is even worse.

I start to take off some of the eyeliner and upon closer inspection notice my eyelashes are crooked and have a crease in them that the eye mask has made. I heat up my eyelash curler with the blow drier and try to re-shape and re-curl my lashes but it isn't working. At best it helps a tiny bit.

I hear the voice of Ashley's annoying friend Ginny. Ginny comes into the bathroom and asks to use my internet for a minute because Ashley is on the computer and Ginny's phone is dying or whatever. I say yes just to get Ginny out of the way. Then my phone rings, so I run into the other room. It might be Penn and I am expecting a call from my doctor, but when I get to my room it is just my mom on the caller ID so I let it ring. I am still holding my eyelash curler in one hand and a cotton ball in the other, and go back into the bathroom.

My phone beeps. Great, now I have to check my voicemail later. I take off my old mascara and try to start over from there and re-curl my lashes again but that fucking doesn't work either. I look at the time. There isn't time to try anything else now anyway. And Ginny better not be breaking my computer or illegally gambling on it or something. The red line on the side of my face is still there. My skin is so damn sensitive. I hope it will fade by the time I drive to Penn's. I decide not to put cover-up over the scab. It will only look all cakey and bad. I do my best to cover the bruise.

I am feeling like a total worthless piece of shit about the fact that what I'd planned to get done by today hasn't gotten done. Only like a third of it. Before rehearsal I planned on going over the notes that I wrote down from last rehearsal, on things I needed to work on during my own time. I have rehearsed the stuff some but wanted to do more. I don't feel completely prepared. Maybe I can postpone the rehearsal but that won't work because then it will be too close to when we are scheduled to go up in class.

I am looking for something to change into but have nothing to wear. All my jeans are getting old but I haven't bought new ones because I don't think I should spend the money, now that I am going to be a starving artist and all. I want to look good for rehearsal, for Penn or Dustin, or at least to not look like total shit. I hate not getting my money's worth with my jeans. Shouldn't they last forever or something? They are practically disintegrating, but since I can't just buy some, I wear the others until they rip. The last pair had ripped at home.

I am holding a pair that is thinning, especially in the butt. But I kind of like that. Maybe I should bring a sweatshirt or something to wrap around me. In case they rip I'll have something to cover myself with. Why do I wear these jeans if I keep worrying and stressing that they are going to rip? Why does everything always have to be falling apart?

I check the time again and put on the thinning-in-the-butt pair of jeans. They work best with my tennis shoes. Since my legs are now aching 24/7 from my hell job, I can't wear any other shoes. I start thinking about all the things I need to do.

I throw my lip gloss and lip moisturizer in my purse. I'll do my lips while driving, and then walk to the front door to leave. I notice an envelope lying on the table when I grab my keys. Shit, is that my credit card bill? I have to make sure I pay it on time. I haven't even opened it yet.

I am driving to Penn's. I am glossing my lips in the car while moving at about three miles per hour on the 10 West. I look to my left and see a guy in the other lane giving me a dirty look, probably because I am doing my makeup. Fuck him. I feel bad enough already. It isn't like I am trying to put on complicated mascara or something equally heinous. I give him the finger where he can't see, by putting my hand low in the car and under the dashboard a little. He deserves it. Lately I find myself doing this more and more.

Penn lives in Santa Monica and driving there is like the only time that I can maybe relax. Except while driving all I can think of is the scene. I keep replaying everything in my head that has gone on between Penn and me. From West Hollywood the drive can take a while. I keep compulsively checking my hair and makeup in the rear-view mirror. And why have I worn this outfit?

I finally pull up to Penn's apartment. He comes outside to move his motorcycle so I can park. I get out of the car with my cut eye. He looks at me.

"Did you get punched?" He asks.

"Some guy opened the soundstage door on my face." This eye situation is embarrassing and doesn't seem like something that would ever happen to a normal person. Inside we go.

I put my stuff down and settle onto the couch. "I thought about the reason I've never had a boyfriend. It's because I don't like to be touched," I say.

"What do you mean? A guy is going to want to touch you and kiss you. You don't like this?" He touches my hand and wrist.

I like it.

"No," I say and hesitate a few moments, then yank my hand away. "By the way, I don't like your girlfriend; she's fat."

"Why are you trying to push my buttons by saying my girlfriend's fat?"

"I'm not trying to push your buttons. I just think she could be more toned."

He looks at me and then gets up and wanders into the

kitchen.

"Do you want some chai-tea?" He asks.

I've never had it before. "No thanks," I say. He takes out two mugs from the cupboard and starts pouring in both mugs. "I said I didn't want any."

He doesn't listen. He looks at me with his eyes saying that he hears, and continues making two anyway.

"I don't want tea!" I say.

He doesn't listen again and remains very calm. I eye his computer and he notices.

"I was watching porn," he says.

But there is no porn on pause.

"Good." I feel uncomfortable. I don't understand the appeal of porn. And I don't like that he is more mature than I am. Since I don't see any remnants of porn on the computer I'm not sure if I believe him.

He hands me a cup of chai-tea. I take a sip and end up drinking it all.

We end up in his room improvising. We'll start the scene when we are ready experientially. He has no furniture since his room is temporary. I sit against the wall by the door and it is annoying to deal with, especially in tight jeans.

"Why did you come back to Strasberg?" I ask.

He gets up and wanders around the room, then mumbles something about needing to do laundry, and then stares into his chai-tea cup and drinks the last of it.

"I said why did you come back?" I ask.

"Do you want a piece of chocolate?" He holds up a candy bar.

I already feel shitty enough. I'm not going to add to it by eating shit and I rarely let myself eat sweets anyway, only on special occasions. I don't eat preservatives which are in the brand he has. I can't imagine eating sweets whenever I want. If I do, I'll never stop eating. I'll be like one of those fish that eat themselves to death because their stomach blows up.

"Why won't you answer my question?" I ask.

"Because I don't think you care. I don't think you really want to know," he says.

"Rourke talks to you like you're a *God* and you don't want to be an actor?"

"I do wanna be an actor. I am an actor," he says. He smiles and continues, "I thought I was forgetting things about the work of Method Acting and I told myself that if I started to forget I would come back. You're wearing makeup. Are you going out tonight?"

"I don't know." I start fidgeting and playing with a piece of my hair, running it through my fingers.

"I like that you do that with your hair."

I stop, kind of to piss him off. And I don't really notice I am doing it until he mentions it. He is good at noticing things like that.

I feel a little envious. I don't want anyone to be more observant than I am. Being observant is very important in acting. I start playing with my hair again except it kind of gets knotted up 'cause I do it so much. So I tuck that one piece behind my ear. Hoping he won't notice that now gross, ratted part.

He says I am 90 percent like other girls and ten percent different. He is always trying to piss me off. And somehow he knows exactly how. I don't want to be like everyone else. I want to be special. Doesn't everyone? I want to know what he thinks is different about me.

"So Ella is like 100 percent original and I'm only 10 percent. So she's better than me?" I ask.

"Ella's not 100 percent original."

"Why don't you just break up with her? She makes you miserable, and I'm tired of hearing about it anyway. I've never heard you say one thing you like about her." As I say this, I wonder if I should be sticking to one subject matter in our improvisation, meaning his roommate.

We talked about her during our first rehearsal. The conversation had provoked me to start the scene.

The rehearsal process started from the minute we saw each other today. We are getting the chemistry going before we actually read the lines of the scene. "Is that why you need to do whatever it is you do with your roommate?" I ask, trying to bring our conversation back to the choice that worked for me last rehearsal.

"You just don't get it. And, you worry too much."

"What the hell, Penn. I'm like pouring my heart out and suddenly you're acting like you don't have a brain. And, quit saying I worry. Someone's gotta fucking do it and obviously it's not gonna be you."

"I do worry and you don't like porn either."

"Quit changing the subject and by the way, yes, I do. I think it's fantastic. I watch it all the time," I say.

"No you don't," he says, kindly and softly. "You don't even like to be touched."

"And then 20 minutes ago I said I don't like to be touched by *most* people. That they have to be special."

Penn looks down at the script in his hand.

I know he wants to do the scene now because he feels like his character. I am ready to do the scene now too because part of me hates him and the other part likes him. I have the first line of the scene so it is always technically up to me when we start. I feel the chemistry. I speak my first line with all the feeling I get from talking to him.

### Blake as Stacy:
### "How could you do this to me?"

I think *I hate you* as I say this.

### Penn as Dustin:
### "So I guess she told you. You look nice."

Penn is just like his character always saying one thing and then doing another. Never goes through with anything.

## Blake as Stacy:
## "You're not even going to try to explain yourself? Or a least apologize."

*Don't you dare try to cute your way out of this, I'm a genius and I never forget a thing.*

## Penn as Dustin:
## "Do you want something to drink?"

Penn sits on the floor. He takes off his T-shirt and drops it next to him, then stares at his chest hair.

## Blake as Stacy:
## "No. And like I would eat or drink anything that came out of this filthy hole. Jenny and I are close."

I think about what he'd said about his roommate: *"We had sex one time; that was nice too,"* to make sure the audience will hear disgust and hurt in my line.

## Penn as Dustin:
## "I know. What is there to say, though? You haven't been around."

He slouches more. He is staring at his stomach now and begins grabbing and pinching his stomach fat even though he doesn't have any. It is more like he is grabbing at his skin.

## Blake as Stacy:
## "I bet she's not even legal."

### Penn as Dustin:
### "It's not like it matters in this state. What do you care anyway?"

He flirts with me. He leans in close and looks down at me for a second. I also see it in his eyes. They focus in on mine.

### Blake as Stacy:
### "I don't care. How long have you been hanging out with Jenny?"

I back away from him.

### Penn as Dustin:
### "You're so quick to think badly of anything you don't understand."

I notice he always embellishes "understand." And it makes me want to throw something at him because he is treating me like a child.

### Blake as Stacy:
### "No, I understand completely."

I put extra inflection in my voice when I say "understand" to get back at him.

### Penn as Dustin:
### "Just because you think it's over doesn't mean it is."

Very often during the scene Penn will look right at me. His eyes are always sparking blue. Literally they sparkle. Aren't men's eyes only supposed to shine like that in the movies? But he never acts like a pretty boy, let alone takes care of himself like one.

In *Forgotten Minds* Penn's character is all depressed and a fucking mess. I assume he is trying to create both of these facts. Penn will make up stories about going into the ocean at the beach instead of showering and he rarely shaves. This doesn't work though, and his stubble is blond and naturally glossy.

After we are done rehearsing, I walk towards the door to leave. From behind, Penn wraps his arms around my waist and kisses me on the cheek. When he lets me go he says, "If we weren't working together I would've kissed you."

"Well, if you were better at improvising I might have believed you." I know he is only saying it for the scene. Still, if he isn't, I don't want a boyfriend. I don't want anything to distract me from my work at school. After I'm a successful actress, then I'll have time for a boyfriend.

I drive home tired. It has been an emotional rehearsal. I am so angry still and hungry and can't stop thinking about Penn's kissing remark. He kissed me soft on the cheek. Such a delicate kiss compared to his crude mouth.

I'm not in the mood to talk to anyone. I am supposed to meet Ashley's work friends at this bar I've never been to on Sunset but now I don't want to go. What am I supposed to say? "I'm super-aggravated from rehearsal and I need to be alone to cool off?"

I feel stupid and embarrassed. At the stop light I turn into the Ralph's shopping center, because there is nothing to eat at home. Maybe I'll say something to Ashley tomorrow about why I hadn't shown.

Three days later Penn and I are on stage in Rourke's class doing our scene for the first time. Penn has created a mess on stage with fliers and business cards all over the floor.

I am worried I am just saying my lines and that they aren't motivated, but I'm not sure. Finally, I use what we call in acting a "rehearsal procedure," and begin to improvise. I talk to Penn as myself and not as my character.

I pick up a business card. It is an ad for a strip club with a slutty, fake-boobed, half-naked girl on it.

"What are these for?" I ask.

"Because you wouldn't understand."

"What wouldn't I understand?" I scream, suddenly furious.

"Look at you." He says not upset at all. In fact, he has a slightly mocking tone.

And that just makes me angrier.

"But why would you say that?" I yell again.

"Just look at you."

I go back into the lines of the scene.

**Blake as Stacy:**
**"You're the one who broke up with me; you ended it."**

**Penn as Dustin:**
**"So I did, I'm not sure what to do now. I don't look good, do I?"**

**Blake as Stacy:**
**"You look like shit. What happened to you?"**

Rourke interrupts us. "I'm sorry, come on down," he says.

This means we are out of time. We both come down off stage and sit in the chairs set up in front of Rourke.

I listen as Penn talks about how the rehearsals went for him. He says things about what happened, including the fact that I am very "secretive." The last thing he tells Rourke is he got the most motivation from when we went on his motorcycle.

I feel a flutter in my chest and am smiling on the inside. But I am sure to keep my poker face on. I don't want to reveal anything.

"Did she like riding on the motorcycle?" Rourke asks

him.

"She liked it," he says smiling. He looks at the floor for a second and then back at Rourke.

I have my eyes and ears glued on both of them.

"How did she look on the bike?" Rourke asks.

Penn smiles again and takes his eyes off Rourke for a second, suddenly shy.

I know Rourke is teaching by suggesting how Penn can increase the chemistry he felt. Is Penn's reaction supposed to mean that he thought I looked really fucking hot? I notice myself hoping so. It is something about the way he doesn't answer and how he looks a little embarrassed. But I'm not sure.

I talk about how the rehearsals went for me, that the first rehearsal I got a lot of feelings from Penn. I give the laundry list to Rourke. I also say I didn't believe Penn most of the time and he would change his story and stuff. Rourke says to challenge him and not let him get away with it. And that Stacy doesn't trust everything Dustin says.

"You're a beautiful leading lady type," Rourke adds this out of the blue. He is always repeating it to me, hoping it will sink in, I guess.

"I know."

"You don't know," he says.

"I'll work on it."

I talk about how the scene went today. I say I didn't know if I needed to go back to the improvisation. Rourke says to test it by going back to the improv and I should know already to go back to the rehearsal procedure when I'm in trouble. Meaning I should have known when the scene became real.

He is right of course and I feel terrible. Why didn't I trust my instincts and go back to the improv sooner? I am pissed at myself. I think, how many times do I have to be told something or do something before I learn? And if I would've gone back to it sooner then I could've gotten farther in the scene. I could've done more advanced work and more of the stuff I practiced in rehearsal, instead of just getting into the thoughts and ideas. I wasted time. We only got through the beginning of the scene. And we didn't get to the transition.

Rourke says that next rehearsal we should improvise more and that the scene had died by the time I brought it in. That whatever thought I was working with in the improvisation definitely worked, this part was good.

Rourke is a complete genius, so when I do something good in his eyes I feel great.

There are some more good things about the scene. Rourke says he definitely saw the attraction between us. I am glad. I also feel like I didn't do much to create the attraction that maybe it was just there, but that doesn't usually happen in acting. It has to be worked for.

I forget to tell Rourke that riding on Penn's motorcycle was totally my idea. I could have gotten extra brownie points. Except it isn't about points and the important thing is that *I* knew it had been my idea and it made the scene better.

Continuing to think about our scene and the fact that it didn't go as well as I wanted, my worries multiply. I feel confident in my acting sometimes but other times feel like I suck, as if I am too shy and only a very, very beginner. Yeah, I can create choices but it is all under prescribed circumstances. At school, I usually know when I am going to be on stage so I will time it accordingly. In the business I won't be able to time it, or there will be too much time or not enough time. No place to prepare or I'll have to prepare in front of other people. I'll have to say the same line with the same emotion and experience, the same the director wants it. Thirty times in a row and I will fail. The line will be stale.

I'll have to do all that while keeping my head tilted a certain way. While using an object the exact same way for the camera, lighting and continuity. Will I be able to get the transition in such short scenes? Be able to create chemistry fast enough? Keep up quality work on an eighteen-hour day? Feel free to move uninhibited in whatever skimpy outfit they put me in? What if the other actors think I am crazy for talking to them or provoking them, and then will I get fired before I even have a chance to fuck up the rest? A thousand other worries are on my mind. Mostly I wonder, will I be able to measure up? Maybe it won't matter because I might never get the part in the first place, to even get a chance to get it right or wrong.

That Friday night I find myself at a bar wondering why I have even come at all. I have rehearsal the next day so it's not like I can even drink. I want to have a clear mind and be normal tomorrow. I had spent a long time getting ready in case Matt or Beth were going to be here. Paranoid I would run into them.

Twenty minutes after I arrive I overhear they aren't coming. My panic comes down a few levels. But then I just feel so tired and am over the entire night. I am currently trying to flirt with this random guy being "the new me" and all. But it is just making me miserable and he is just gross.

"We should hop in a Jacuzzi one night. You'd wear a bikini," he says.

I can't believe he is actually being serious with what he is saying. I can't find anything I like about him and hate wasting all my energy in something that isn't even in my nature.

Across the room I notice two people have just walked away from Jade so I get the hell out of talking to the random guy and head over to her. Jade is a drug-addict mess, and Rourke always reminds her of that fact. But he also always says she is talented. It isn't fair. She doesn't even have to try. It makes me so envious. I've been kind of a wreck since my scene with Penn went badly in class and am looking for some guidance. Or maybe I just want to pick Jade's brain for what she knows.

"I liked your improv today. I was moved," I say after greeting Jade. Earlier in the day at school Jade had done an improv about suicide. In the scene she asked her boyfriend, "Am I on TV or in the movies?" arguing in favor of suicide. Because she wasn't those things, she wanted to die.

Even though I am ashamed of it, I can relate to what Jade said and felt. Rourke had torn her a new one after the improv for her lack of doing anything except barely showing up, but he also went on about her talent. Then again, about how much she wastes it.

Jade says that I've come out of my shell but that I still have a lot of excuses about why I can't do something in a scene. Her advice is just to do it. Stop making excuses.

If only I can be more like Jade. She doesn't seem to be self-conscious about doing anything on stage. I remember another time when Rourke raved about Jade's talent and the fact that she was available emotionally on all levels. All of this makes a big part of me hate her.

# 5.  RUNNING WITH SCISSORS

On Saturday morning I am at the gym and in a hurry because I have to get home and clean my place, since we are rehearsing at my apartment. I am already having a bad day before I even see Matt and Beth. I've got on the treadmill to do cardio and picked one that doesn't have trash in the cup holes so I can put my water and stuff in it.

After I get all settled, I see a guy reading a script to the left of me. I can't help but try to see what the script is for. I think it reads *Grey's Anatomy* at the top. I've seen people reading scripts while working out before and it always pisses me off or upset me. I want to relax at the gym, not be reminded of my auditioning issues and the fact that everyone is further ahead of me. And then, to freaking make matters worse, to the right of me in my peripheral vision I see Matt and Beth.

Beth just stands on the treadmill, even though it is turned off. Matt is flirting with her of course. He leans in as he talks to her the way he always does, and touching her arm every so often. She is talking her head off and pretending to be oblivious to it all.

I feel sick. What the fuck is going on? Maybe I can't get away from Matt because he flirts and does inappropriate things with every girl in school.

But still, there is the whole script-reading guy, as if people have to do two productive things at once because one isn't good enough. I spend the rest of my run pretending that I haven't seen Matt and Beth and that the *Grey's Anatomy* script guy isn't there. Since I have practically nowhere to look but down, I stare at my feet, but my running shoes aren't nearly as nice as the ones Beth is wearing. Then I mentally tell the guy with the script to fuck off and to quit shoving his big, fancy, guest-starring part or whatever in my face.

Why do Matt and Beth have to be everywhere? When I see them I want to work out less. I suddenly loose all my energy. I always feel extra low self confidence at the gym to begin with, being all sweaty and splotchy with no makeup on, but I won't dare leave. That would mean they won, and I don't want them to drive me out of my own gym. If only I could go home, get under my covers, and cry for days. But I won't let myself do that either, so I stay. For a moment I can't help imagining them having sex the night before and then try to put that gut-wrenching image out of my mind.

I work out longer then I plan after Matt and Beth leave, getting out my anger or stress or something. Before I know it, I am rushing home again and miss the two-hour free parking window. I have to pay to get out of the goddamn lot.

I rush into the shower and rush out. By the time rehearsal starts I am holding my stomach in pain. That is where I tend to feel stress and anxiety. I move one hand over my stomach, trying to soothe the icky feeling.

Rehearsals are very long and draining. Rourke wants

three hours but sometimes Penn and I will go a little longer than that. As usual we plan to improv and then start the scene.

"How was your day so far?" Penn asks.

"I don't wanna talk about it."

"Oh. Okay, I guess. Usually girls get mad if you don't ask about their day."

"Well, you don't have to ask me," I say.

"Good then. How are your squats going?"

He is referring to my thighs. Last rehearsal he said he liked them. I don't know what to make of it. Matt had never complimented my thighs before. I didn't know guys cared about thighs.

"Great," I say smiling. I decide I like talking about my thighs now. The lyrics to an AC/DC song play in my head: *Knockin' me out with those American thighs.* Maybe guys do care about thighs after all.

During rehearsal, I find Penn slowly getting closer. It is so slow I don't move away. I sit leaning against the pillows on my made bed and he somehow worms his way so he is lying on his back on the bed, with the top of his head touching my outer thigh, as well as the tips of his fingers touching my outer thigh above my knee. I wear jeans. I look at him and he moves his hand away, but when I look away as I talk it will return for a second.

When I look down at him, I just keep seeing blue and blond and skin that looks as though he's just had a facial. I can see and examine every inch of his face, he is so close to me. Plus, he will never say anything like, "Why do you keep staring at me?" I conclude he is perfect. Well, his face is.

"What did the house you grew up in look like?" Penn asks.

"Why are you asking me that?"

"Why do you always ask why? I want to know what your life was like."

I answer and describe my house. It is such a specific

question I think again he has some plot or scheme going for the scene and that he doesn't *really* care. I am trying to create care for the scene, because the telling off in the scene comes from care. Stacy cares about Dustin. And if Penn cares about me, I might be able to care about him. But no matter what he does I am managing to find ways to work it into the scene. Well of course that's what I am doing. That is my job.

Penn goes on to talk about two things, mostly. His ex, or maybe his non-ex Ella, I still am not quite sure. And this new girl named Roxanne he has never mentioned before that is in one of our classes at Strasberg. He says he slept with her recently.

"Why are you having sex with her?" I can't help asking.

"You wouldn't understand anyway since you don't like to be touched."

I feel a sting in my chest. I get up off the bed with my script in hand. It is time to start the scene.

After rehearsal, I worry whether I had committed to my choices enough. I have to figure out what I am going to do with a lot of the lines in the scene. I am glad it isn't our turn to act in class for a while because I still have lots to work on.

The next Friday I am in Improvisation class mustering up the strength to watch Matt do an improv with Jade.

About eighty of my feelings toward Jade are hatred. The rest are admiration or jealousy since Rourke always goes on about her talent. He also always goes on about her lack of discipline, focus, work ethic and her alcoholism. I consider her a threat because of her talent. But I am also kind of happy she is such a fucking mess; that way she won't likely get further than I do.

Recently I loath Jade even more than usual because of her improvs with Matt. Every damn improv they are sticking their tongues down each others throats. In their last improv Jade wore this silky nightgown lingerie thing with no bra, and Matt kept touching her and rubbing his face all over her.

Horrified, I sat in the audience. Underneath the horror, I felt jealous and disgusted at the same time throughout their entire improv.

Today, Matt and Jade are going to do their fourth improv on the topic of love.

Dreading the torture makes me want to drop out of Strasberg. I am preparing myself for the worst after what I saw of their first three improvisations.

Matt and Jade do their fourth improv. I watch, barely able to breathe. Thank God the scene is like watching a G-rated movie compared to before. Their improv is a different topic and scenario after all. It isn't nearly as bad as the grope-fest I'd witnessed before. I don't get as upset as I thought I might, but still feel exhausted from the entire situation and the anticipation of hell.

Lately, I stopped hanging out with people from Strasberg, mostly because of Matt and because I don't want to get to know all the students. I don't want to hear his name mentioned or see anyone that knows him or reminds me of him. I also don't want knowing too many people to affect my acting. In the acting business I won't be meeting the people I work with ahead of time. The school is not set up like that, but it should be. The students are supposed to be strangers before they get assigned a scene together.

Matt is in half my classes, so I can't get away from him. Except, when you really get down to it, yeah, he is in my classes, but never actually *in* class, and that makes me even madder. When he isn't there literally, I'll still think about him because there is the possibility he could show up at any second. He'll come at the beginning but will always leave class to smoke cigarettes or talk to someone or God knows what. I'll see him through the window, walking back and forth.

It's so sad and so disgusting that he is such a damn slave to cigarettes. In the times when he does stay in class until the break, he will be so antsy to go out and smoke that he'll have a cigarette ready in his hand and his lighter out. So freaking weak, always saying he will quit.

I love that Penn says smoking's so unattractive. But then again why would he sleep with Roxanne? She smokes. I've seen her smoking at school. Plus it is a dirty skank thing to do. I hate that he will go against his morals and integrity about smoking for her. But maybe he isn't. Maybe he is lying.

Anyway, maybe if Matt wasn't everywhere I could get over him. Every time I see him all the feelings will come rushing back. Because he is everywhere, I have no chance of that "out of sight, out of mind" thing to even work.

Sunday morning I check my voicemails. I have a message from Penn about scheduling rehearsal. He says he can rehearse Monday but Tuesday is better because he wants to figure out something for the scene ahead of time. It is so responsible of him and he is very dedicated to the work. Sadly, I find it rare people rehearsing on their own, other than me. Especially someone detailing a problem with the scene they're working on. That's pretty much unheard-of, other than me again.

I call him back and we schedule rehearsal for Tuesday.

For our scene I'm not sure what choice to use for the cousin or if I should keep using Roxanne. I keep changing my choice even though I shouldn't but I just want to make the scene better. It is almost like the problem is there are too many to choose from. There are so many things about Penn. The fact that he is a liar, the fact he always tries to trick me, the degrading ways he talks about women and sex, and the way he acts like nothing he does is wrong.

Penn doesn't feel the same way I feel about Method Acting. He completely and utterly loves it and will go on about it.

"I hate it," I will say 'cause sometimes I do hate it a little. The more I act and learn about the work the more secretive it seems I have to be. I can't talk about my choices and then the stuff I can talk about will be generic. In life, as opposed to being in rehearsal, I end up not wanting to talk about anything because it will get me so riled up. Mostly I hate having to work on a scene that involves me thinking about Matt, and then do it with him in the fucking audience. It just makes everything harder. Puts more pressure on me and makes me more self conscious. But almost all the time I won't or can't talk about my choices and ideas because the scene is going on. Or I am using a similar choice for a different scene. So even if the scene is over I can't talk about it.

And again, what if I need to use the choice in a different scene later on? It sucks I can't talk about my favorite thing. It makes me feel lonely and that my whole life is a lie, 'cause most of it is. Also the left-over feelings after a scene are a bitch to deal with. Maybe I need a break. It is fucking tiring, always trying to build something up and make it more personal. Or if I mess up and it isn't personal I feel like a failure and this blows too. Penn sees the cheery and happy side to everything. What is with that? I'm not used to it.

# 6. THE PLAYER

Monday, at 7:49 a.m. I arrive at school. I wear my favorite pair of boots, the ones that I've just picked up at the repair shop but I am slipping in them now; the tread must be wearing off. I'd got them fixed because the stitching and leather was falling apart on the sides, probably from when it rained hard that one time and they got really wet, or maybe from wearing them so often. Now I will have to take them back again to get new tread put on or just throw them in the trash.

The first time today I slid in them, I almost fell. I'd feel like crying, but held it together since I was in the middle of the school lobby after all.

That night Penn and I walk into an empty classroom to rehearse. I've had a lot of classes today and am tired again, plus I am feeling extra cranky because Beth has gotten a new layered hair cut and has been showing it off to everyone. I'd wanted to rip it out. Tuesdays still tend to suck the most. It makes me think about what to change about my looks that will make Matt regret his decision and want me again. Should I dress down or should I dress up or act super bubbly all the time or buy some kind of new volumizer for my roots? I'd racked my brain during an entire class break about what to do.

"What do you think about Beth?" I ask, desperate. I assume Penn will just think that I know Beth from class and not because she is my arch-enemy for several reasons.

"I don't think her focus is in the right place," he says.

I agree and like his answer, but it would've been better if he said she is a stupid bitch.

"What do you think about her looks?" I ask.

"She has a really square face."

Ahh. It is like music to my ears.

Penn talks about how he messed up a scene in one of Rourke's classes and Rourke let him know it. I didn't have that class with him so I hadn't seen what happened.

Penn drops his head down and shakes it.

I love how he feels, ashamed, down and like crap if he slaughters a scene. That his failure stays on his mind, just like me.

I've been thinking a lot about our scene and am feeling really anxious. I feel a lot of pressure to get the scene provoked, improved, personal, in touch with my rage, sure I am behaving it, commit to my choices and a million other things. Including trusting myself when I think the scene is motivated.

It is absolutely adorable the way Penn talks about his improv. I just want to ask him more about it. I felt the exact same way a thousand times before and can't believe that he feels the same way too. But I need to create the tension, instead of the attraction at the moment, so I begin to motivate it in myself.

"Have you seen Roxanne lately?" I ask.

"Not since I last saw you. Why don't you ever wear a

dress?"

Can I work that in with the wanting to be touched idea we have been using? I am supposed to see if the attraction can be more personalized, Rourke had told me. Yes, I can start the beginning part of the scene in a few minutes. Rehearsals are very complicated as well as overwhelming, a lot.

"Are you saying you want to see me in a dress?" I ask.

"What do you think?"

"I think you couldn't give me a straight answer if your life depended on it," I say.

"Yeah, I want to see you in a dress. You know, you should flirt more. Roxanne flirts with everyone."

"Why are you always trying to change me? Why can't you like me the way I am?"

"I do. I just think you should flirt more, but since you don't like to be touched..."

"No, I don't."

"At least Roxanne likes to be touched."

"Yeah a little too much if you know what I mean. I just hope you're using a condom if you are even really having sex with her. Which I don't believe you are," I say.

I speak the first line of the scene to test it.

### Blake as Stacy:
### "How could you do this to me?"

I don't like how it feels. It seems phony and unmotivated. I say the line again to see if this time I can make it real to me.

### Blake as Stacy:
### "How could you do this to me?"

I think *go to hell* as I say the line.

I am unhappy; it is inauthentic again. I go back to the

improv hoping to create some believability. What is wrong? Why aren't I getting provoked, why doesn't it feel personal enough? I begin to freak out. Am I a terrible actor after all?

"I don't know what to say," I say.

I worry I don't care about the Roxanne situation anymore. That maybe it was just a fluke or something. My stomach starts to cramp, I grip it without realizing what I am doing, pressing my hand over the most painful part. It is getting worse.

"What's wrong?" Penn asks.

"Nothing." My stomach burns, I think, because sometimes I worry too much. I can't believe I'm getting distracted right when I'm having problems with the scene. I don't want to do *Forgotten Minds* anymore. I want to go home and sleep. What if my mind is sabotaging me? I'd be better off if I was like the play title and my mind could be forgotten, and my heart could rule me instead.

I sit cross-legged on the wooden stage. I lean forward a little, switching positions to ease the pain. Maybe I haven't eaten enough today and am just hungry? There is a half-eaten protein bar in my purse, I think, but it is the kind I hate and is too gross to eat because it tastes like rubber. That is why I can never finish those.

"Are you okay?" Penn asks.

"Yes."

"Why is your stomach always hurting?"

"I don't know."

"Lie down. I'll put my hand on it and heal it with energy. All people have the power to use energy to heal; they just have to be taught how to use it," Penn says.

I want to say yes. "No. Are you being serious? That's stupid."

"You don't have to believe in it for it to work."

"Is this like some meditation thing you do?"

"It's different but the same idea. Lie down."

I don't have any Tylenol for my pain, but even if I did, it

wouldn't work. I don't want him to feel my stomach because it is bloated and looks huge. I am afraid he will toss me aside since I'm not in shape and can almost be the dreaded word "fat." My enlarged stomach comes from food allergies, I assume. What else can it be? Anger washes over me at this medical problem that no ones acknowledged, so I have to diagnose it myself. One more thing I have to do myself, or it never gets done.

Humiliated, I hate my body. I've been eating crap the last few days. I don't know what I've eaten to make it bloat. This never used to happen to me. A few months ago I tried cutting out foods to see what was doing it, but nothing helped.

"Come on, energy comes through the other person's hands onto the wounded body. I'm not anything like a master but I know enough."

I want to try it so bad but can't let him touch me. He will know about my stomach and I'll be instantly demoralized. I'd rather live with shooting pains in my gut for the rest of my life, pains that I can only compare to contractions. What will I be worth if he knows? I am worthless anyway, basically a strange kind of fat with this allergy but at least I am able to hide it from Penn.

I've been going out of my way and spending so much time dressing to cover my mid-section, I wear a babydoll tank top that is loose-fitting in the stomach but still cute so I will look good, or as good as I can. It is so nice he offered though. I've never met a caring guy before. Penn is probably thinking I won't lie down because I don't like to be touched, but that's not why. I won't because of what I said before: a guy has to be special and I also have to feel comfortable, which I never do.

"It's sometimes called Healing Touch, if you've ever heard of it."

"No," I lie. He's not letting this go. He doesn't give up easily and it's one of the things I like about him.

"But what are you going to do?" I am just stalling. This is never going to happen. If my body was the way it was before, only then I'll be worth it.

"I'll just put my positive energy into you with my hand where you're hurting. People have done it for centuries."

One part of me was ready to jump in the minute he suggested it. If only it weren't for the distention. I can't bear the embarrassment, losing my desire and femininity, my worth, any reason left to be human.

"I can help," he says.

Penn seems so intent on getting his way. I think of that model from New York in one of my classes and envy her. She has no reason to be ashamed of her body, which really means no reason to be ashamed period. Maybe if I was her I could enjoy getting healed instead of being so on guard just talking about it. I can't help but stare at her every break because she buys a Snickers bar from 7-Eleven across the street and eats it with a non-diet soda every week *like it's no big deal.* She doesn't have an ounce of fat on her and is like 5' 10". Her pants always fall inches too short because the skinny ones that fit her aren't made in her length. The hem stops at the bottom of her calves. It's her genetics. She can eat whatever she wants and never exercise. I have to do the opposite or I'll gain weight. I've never let myself be envious of her before; it would make me weak. I would tell myself I can have my body be however I want if I try hard enough, but now the jealousy tears me to pieces.

If I let him touch me...what if I twitched? It's happened before. I can't stand how disgusting I am any longer. I am going to cut out three times as many foods now in order to get my abdomen back to normal. My hair feels flatter and greasier, my jeans tighter around my thighs signaling I'm not exercising enough or have gotten weak with my diet, my boobs nonexistent, as if I were a man. My face is ugly and forgettable no matter how much makeup I wear or how perfect I apply it. What if I start to cry?

My body begins to move to get in position. I roll onto my back, but my mind is resisting, *say no*. I try to calm myself by remembering I've told Penn about my food allergies. He knows this is a medical problem and not something I can control. I am not lazy and worthless. That feeling that wants this so bad has taken over me and it's not coming from how I physically look, it's coming from some pull or energy through out my whole body. Something I don't understand.

"I feel retarded," I say as I stare at the ceiling. I take shallow breaths, because if there is less air in my stomach it will look smaller.

He sits next to me and puts his hand on my stomach over my shirt. "This is—"

I stop talking when his hand meets my stomach and my already clenched body tightens. I don't notice a change in his facial expression like I thought I would. As if he would suddenly know the strangeness of me that I can't hide with strategic baggy clothes anymore. Did he never think I had a flat stomach to begin with? I wait, holding my breath.

His hand lightly rests on me. His fingers are spread out. I don't know where to look so I look at his face. He stares at my stomach. Penn closes his eyes and I don't know if I feel like laughing or feel comforted. I think maybe I should start to make fun of him but he looks very serious. I hold my laughter. His hand raises on my diaphragm with each breath I take. My tension grows.

"First I take a few moments and let you get used to me," he keeps his eyes closed.

"Am I supposed to do something?"

"No, you don't have to do anything. Well if you can, try to receive me, but either way you'll be receiving."

I am heating up and fear I'll start to sweat. I have to stop taking shallow breaths or I'll choke.

"I'm almost done. You don't have to stay so still, you can move a little."

"Oh, sorry." I can't tell how much time has gone by.

He opens his eyes and I get more nervous because there he is. I take in his movie star face and strong muscular shoulders. Is he going to notice now that he can see me taking deeper breaths? But nothing he does signals he notices anything about my size. It is more like he is looking inside my stomach and not at it. He is so serious. Maybe that is where the "chi" is? I think that's what it's called; he mentioned it once. He concentrates and keeps his hand there for another minute. Finally, he gently takes it off.

I don't end up sweating but am glad it is over. That other part of me, though, that I can't understand, doesn't want his hand to leave. I sit back up.

"It didn't work," I declare.

"It takes a little while. See how you feel in twenty minutes." He flashes his devilish smile.

Penn starts telling a ridiculous story about some stripper that hit on him last time he was in L.A. and how they hung out and hooked up, but didn't have sex because according to him it was "just oral." He describes how she took off her clothes very slowly for him before they got in the shower.

"I don't want to hear the story. Shut up about it!" I yell.

He makes a face at my loud voice and then continues.

"We got in the shower—"

"I'm going to like throw up on these wood floors if you keep talking," I say interrupting him. "Why do you always bring up these gross stories about your sex life?"

"I don't know. I really want to tell you these things."

"You're such a liar," I say.

Even not believing him I am feeling a major sting in my chest, major jealousy, confusion and appalledness, if that's a word.

"This really happened," he says.

I hate him presently and feel the same way Stacy feels about Dustin. So I speak my first line again.

## Blake as Stacy:
## "How could you do this to me?"

*You're not a good man.*

## Penn as Dustin:
## "So I guess she told you. You look nice."

Penn walks away from me as he says his line, turning back, he looks me up and down.

We go through the entire scene without going back to the improv. It is beautiful.

After rehearsal we walk downstairs heading to the lobby.

"You know, it's been a whole two hours since you complained about your stomach hurting," Penn says.

"It's burning really bad. I was just trying not to annoy you," I lie.

"Yeah, I bet you were," he says with that sarcastic hint he sometimes uses.

Over the next few weeks I find myself not caring as much about my other scenes. Well, at least at first. I will force myself to work on them but then always get engrossed, but my favorite thing is when I can work on *Forgotten Minds*. I find Penn intensely interesting even though he makes me so mad, among a lot of other bad feelings.

At school, I notice a new printed flyer taped to the wall. I get instantly nervous. It is a sign for an agent showcase. I ask Mary, the front desk girl, about it. She says that Ron O'Farrell, a name I recognize from The Actors Studio, will be judging the last audition. An old teacher of mine would talk about Ron O'Farrell. That's why I've heard of him.

Mary says there are three auditions altogether. You have

to pass the first two auditions to get the final audition, and then pass the final audition to make it into the showcase. The chosen actors will be paired up to do scenes in front of the agents that come to the showcase in hopes that the actors will get signed. A wave of panic rises in my body and mind just hearing about it. Before I even sign up I image being in front of such "important" people. The panic continues to rise.

I am a little relaxed being at rehearsal tonight with Penn. It seems so routine and normal. I feel a little happy. The shock of seeing the showcase sign has died down and I am myself again. We are at his place and the lone lamp in his room is dim.

"You know what you're like? *The Road Not Taken* poem by Robert Frost. You remind me of it," Penn says.

I make an unhappy face.

"What? Why are you frowning? Why are you making that face?" he says.

George told me the same thing two days ago before class when I asked about the scene schedule. He said that's what he thought of me. What a big coincidence. The poem seems to mean I am so special, so great, so unique and all that, but at this point I am kind of sick of hearing it unless it is a means to an end. Or I get some prize or reward or an acting job. I want the payoff to my hard work, something to *show* for the specialness. I have nothing. I don't even know what the poem means, other than the person basically takes the more difficult or unusual road and in the end things work out better because of it. I want my better.

"George just told me that I seem like the road less traveled poem. What does that mean? That I'm weird and awkward?" I reply.

"That I respect you."

"Okay."

I don't understand why he keeps saying that he respects

me. This is probably the fifth time he brought it up. Was that supposed to be some kind of compliment? He should say I'm beautiful, he likes me or that I'm a great actor. *Respect* seems like what you say to an ugly person.

"You know I'm leaving in six weeks? Are you gonna miss me?" Penn says with his hand by his face while one finger is stroking a shiny blond eyebrow.

I can't believe him. That he even brings up missing him. How selfish and egotistical! Like he wants me to fall on my knees and say I can't live without him. I told him right from the start that we weren't going to be friends.

I don't want anyone else to leave that I am at all close to. There are a lot of international students at school and at first I would get to know them all, but they would stay six months, or less than a year, and then leave. So I stopped talking to any international students since I picked up some sense. Plus, six weeks seems like so long from now. I can deal with it later.

Thinking about the future makes me think about the showcase and when it is coming up and how I will have to start checking my email, organize my email, figure out my work schedule, probably request the day off, get my life together and do a million other things by then. So I try to not think about it.

"No. You'll leave and I'll forget you immediately," I reply. I feel sad. I don't like that he brought up the subject of *Forgotten Minds* ending and him not living in L.A. anymore. Maybe I can use him leaving and abandoning the scene, and practically ruining my acting career in the process, as the choice for the cousin.

He starts talking about that Roxanne girl at school he is having sex with. She is too young for him and I am jealous that he likes Roxanne more than me. I feel like everything he says is for the scene and I can't trust his words. I have to know what kind of person he really is. He will be an asshole but then he will hold my hand, or more like grip it because I will always try to pull it away. He will look into my eyes and say that my scenes are the only ones he enjoys watching at school.

"You're really having sex with her?" I ask.

"Yeah I am."

"She's a slut," I say.

"She is a slut," he says, and seems disgusted.

I love that he calls Roxanne a slut and that he says it in a way that means he doesn't like sluts. It warms my heart a little. But I still feel unsure about him. Why would he have sex with someone he has so little respect for? I know why: because Roxanne is beautiful, hot, has big boobs and probably a sexier body than I do.

"She dresses like a hooker," I say.

He has the audacity to laugh and smile his beautiful smile at me instead of getting offended like he is supposed to.

"You're an exotic beauty," Penn says.

I look at him.

"You didn't say anything," Penn says.

"Oh. Well then, you're changing the subject."

"You're supposed to say thank you."

"Thanks," I said meek.

"You seem mad."

"I'm not." Why does he always have to tease me?

"Do you believe me when I say you're beautiful?" he asks.

"Well you don't have a great reputation with being honest."

"I'm not lying. You're just looking for an excuse not to believe me, because you don't know you're beautiful," he says.

I guess my excuse doesn't work at all. "People tell me I'm beautiful all the time."

"But do *you* think you're beautiful?"

"Of course," I lie and start running my fingers through

my hair. When is this conversation going to be over?

"I don't believe you," he says.

"Fine, but I'm telling the truth."

Penn goes on to talk about another girl that he apparently had sex with in the past but was too grossed out to kiss. Is he telling me all this to get the piece-of-shitness that is his character Dustin? Because it doesn't seem like him and I still don't really believe him. I think maybe he is just trying to make himself sound terrible and like a piece of shit on purpose. He goes on and on about how he loves American strip clubs. That where he is from in Switzerland the strip clubs are gross and the girls aren't happy. That in California, the girls have fun and put on a show. I question that also because he is too smart to think they are actually freaking happy to be there.

"Will you shut about strip clubs already. You're making me sick!" I say.

He continues on, adding more detail.

"I bet your girlfriend is cheating on you and having sex with every guy she sees now that you're gone," I say.

"Probably," he mumbles.

I have the urge to strangle him so I speak the first line of the scene.

We go through the scene twice.

Penn starts to give me a hug goodbye but this time he gives me a kiss on the cheek first. It is a very soft, very gentle kiss. His lips barely touch my skin. Then we hug. I start to pull away after a moment but he stays hugging me. So I stay too.

The next day at school I have my eye on Beth. She sits in the lobby with her iPhone at her ear, listening to what seems like a voicemail. She is hunched over a little writing something down on a small scrap of paper. Did she just get an audition? I steam with envy again. I wonder what the audition is for, or how much notice people get for auditions, a few hours or no notice or a day or a few days?

What if I don't have a pen or paper with me? My phone is dead or a bunch of other things go wrong in the future when someone calls me with an audition?

Beth usually seems to be on the phone when no one else is near by, like she doesn't want people to hear her or something. Does she get worried if she will even *find* the audition place, or if it will mess up her day if she is scheduled to work at the same time? I wish I could be in Beth's place with my own career. I look around at the school lobby wondering if I should be here, somewhere else, or if it is all a colossal waste of time.

# 7. ANYWHERE BUT HERE

I sit on one of the not-very-comfortable benches pretending to be playing with and interested in Mary's smelly little dog. I am desperate to do anything to avoid Matt's douchebag behavior. He is sitting in one of the chairs across the room about twenty feet from me flirting with a woman. Class starts in five minutes, but it feels like I have to sit here for another hour.

For a while after Matt left me I would just go up to class early to avoid as much contact with him as possible, but I don't want to do that anymore because then I'll have to completely isolate myself from everyone at school, looking like a rude bitch in the process. That's why I am in the current situation I am in, faking I like dogs. Mary hasn't ever brought the dog to school before, so it makes sense that I can fake caring about it today. I just can't sit and watch Matt flirt with yet another woman.

I lightly touch the tips of my fingers to the dog's mangy

coat, hating my life. I continue to use as little a part of my hand to actually make contact with the dog. The fur feels sticky and I think I feel a piece of a dried leaf stuck in it. I estimate how many more seconds or minutes I will have to do this. I can't wait to get to the bathroom to scrub my hands, even though I only used my fingers, in warm soapy water to get off the stench that will most likely be lingering there, and to kill any germs.

I overhear Matt talk to the older women next to him. I can see nothing interesting about her. "You're not wearing a bra?" Matt says as he looks down at the woman's chest. He is such a cliché. The woman wears an ugly shirt in this bad red color with her nipples showing. I continue to pet the dirty animal that isn't even a puppy. Can I get more pathetic? This is my sad life, hiding from a loser.

"Is he a rescue dog?" I say hating that I am still affected by everything Matt says and does. I continue chatting it up with Mary about how long she's had the dog and all that.

Finally, it is time for class. The first read starts. I loose myself in acting and in listening to Rourke interact with the students on stage and forget about Matt for the time being.

I am still upstairs, finishing taking notes after class, trying to hide from Matt and the other students. I can't concentrate on writing when everyone is around me talking. I'm not finished but have to go downstairs because some other people are coming into the room to rehearse. When I get downstairs, I wish I had another place to hide. Someone reads *Backstage West,* an article titled "How to Get Your Agent to Notice You," or something stupid like that and equally ridiculous. Someone else talks about how he danced on his last audition. So now I have to know how to act and *dance*? Then I think about singing. Do I have to be good at everything? Someone else thumbs through headshots. I am always too embarrassed to show mine to anyone. Doesn't this stuff freak other people out? Then why do they act so casual about it? Some other people talk about the latest quote-celebrity-unquote they saw, acting excited about it. I hate seeing *celebrities*. They make me feel like a loser, reminding me of my nonexistent acting career, and that my life is crap. I remember when Angelina Jolie was spotted at Whole Foods across the street. I had to hear about it from three different people.

We rehearse at Penn's apartment six and a half hours later. In his room, I sit on the floor as usual. He has brought up the topic of his new guitar and I've been trying to shut him up about it. Thinking that it has absolutely nothing to do with anything and is all wasting my time. He says it was very expensive. For a moment I think that Penn loves his guitar more than he loves Ella. He fucking touches it like he wants to make love to it. He rarely even talks about Ella. For a second, I wish I am that guitar. It lies resting in his arms. He looks down at it proud and as if it is one of the most beautiful things he's ever seen.

Why isn't he paying more attention to *me?* Yes, the scene is about me caring for him so my thoughts are okay but it is also about other things.

"What would you do if I grabbed your guitar right now, slammed it on the ground and then through it out the window," I say. I still sit on the floor.

"I'm gonna stay over here with it," he tightens his arms around it.

"Have you seen Roxanne the skank lately?"

"I'm still thinking about the fact you suggested my guitar getting smashed."

"I think you spent too much money on it," I say.

"Roxanne bought it for me."

I want to tell him not to ever lie to me and that I don't believe him but it is time to bring in the lines of the scene. I am provoked and this feels very personal. I start the scene midway, as that is the part I need to work on.

### Blake as Stacy:
### "No, I understand completely."

I get up and walk around his empty room. It is a little pathetic that he doesn't have much stuff.

### Penn as Dustin:
### "Just because you think it's over doesn't mean it is."

He says this using a loving, tender, hurt voice but it isn't working on me. In fact it only infuriates me more.

### Blake as Stacy:
### "You're the one who broke up with me; you ended it."

I think to myself *I hate you* as I say this because I've written it next to the printed line on the script. It brings Stacy and me together. It makes the line even more real to me, connects me even more with experiencing the relationship and the situation going on in the scene.

We go through the entire scene twice.

I think the rehearsal went okay but to be sure, I am going to go over a few things afterward. But when I get home I feel wiped out. I lie down on my bed and am asleep within four minutes. I am still in my clothes and bra and haven't brushed my teeth or washed my face.

A few days later Penn and I are rehearsing again at school, starting with improvisation. It is the day before we are going to perform the scene in class, which is bad. We aren't supposed to do that. It doesn't give me enough time to work with what I get from rehearsal on my own. And for what happens in rehearsal to sink in. Why hadn't I scheduled the rehearsal better? We did have prior rehearsals that were spaced well that I feel good about. Still, it is wrong to rehearse so last-minute and to not plan better. I agreed to rehearse anyway to be extra thorough.

"I'm tired of wearing shoes that hurt my feet," I pull off a stiletto ankle boot. I start pulling off the other when Penn reaches for it and finishes taking it off.

"I don't mind you barefoot."

"And I told you to stop saying I'm secretive. I'm not secretive at all," I say.

"Yes, you are."

"I just need to spend a lot of time alone."

"So do I," he says. I can't believe it. It makes me feel so good. I thought he was going to say the opposite, that I'm a freak. It is really nice to be completely understood for once.

"I think George is in love with me," I say.

"I know that's something you shared with me."

I am taken aback by what he says and the way he says it. Like it feels good to him that I shared something about my life, that he wants to know things and is glad when I tell him. I have felt a little bad that maybe I did something wrong. That not sharing is something he doesn't like about me. I don't want that.

"I'm sorry I don't share more but maybe if you ever told me the truth or kept your stories straight I would," I declare.

He would always twist things. Like he said he liked my thighs and then a rehearsal or two later said he compliments girls to get them to blush and see their reaction, the stupid fuck. What the hell am I supposed to believe? The rude part, of course; tricking girls is the real thing.

It is the second time we are going to perform the scene in class, which makes me feel anxious and nervous. This tends to happen before scenes. I usually told myself I just had to do the scene and then I could quit acting altogether afterward, but the scene would never turn out nearly as disastrous as I thought it would. So I keep going, and remind myself it is good having a mirror in my work – meaning Rourke – to judge my progress because when I try to do it for myself, it is always so distorted. Rourke will always set me straight, tell me what is great, good, and what is a problem.

I have the first line so I am the one who will start the scene. On stage I start. I hope to have enough motivation from the short improv. I still am not positive the improv is personal enough but I am trying to trust my instincts. Be confident, ever since I'd hated how it went the last time we performed on stage. The scene is going well for me but then Penn goes back to the improv.

"You don't like to be touched," he says. This isn't a line in the scene so I know we are improvising.

"For the thousandth fucking time I said that I don't like to be touched by *most people!*" I reply.

"You don't like porn. You don't like to be touched."

"You don't listen!"

The improv goes on for a few minutes before Penn goes back to his line, I am glad. I thought *I* was ready and was mad that he went back to the improvisation in the first place, but he must have needed it for his craft.

We get down off stage. Thinking the scene went pretty well after all, I am excited to tell Rourke about it. How the rehearsals went. What I did, the problems I encountered during the rehearsal process as well as ask him the questions I had. Penn and Rourke discuss Penn's part, and then we get to my part.

It turns out all my worries about when to go to the improv and testing the lines was a waste. That isn't the problem at all this time. Rourke says that all went fine. He says the problem was when I got angry with Penn. I'd been wearing *away* the feeling by moving so much instead of speaking *with* the feeling. I'd kept moving around all over the stage trying to calm myself down instead of using all of the anger I'd built up from working with Penn. This feels very overwhelming but exciting and challenging at the same time, like an "aha" moment. Now I know better and next time it's going to be really genius. Rourke does say I was very provoked. The preparation worked and I committed fully to my ideas. I used to have problems with all this.

"It's good you're making all the mistakes here at school because you're learning. I wish a lot of other people would mess up as many scenes as you have," Rourke says to me.

Coming from Rourke, who will only accept the best, this is his version of a compliment. But I want an ending, a completion, an understanding instead of just *another* problem that needs to be fixed with a rehearsal procedure. And maybe by now I do want an actual compliment. My work is still not enough. I am glad I've fixed the main original problem by using the improv when necessary, but with a whole new issue to deal with, it never seems to end. It is fine but I hoped I'd be confident in my acting after this scene. Now I just feel I know less than before.

Penn and I are done discussing *Forgotten Minds* with Rourke so I go back to my seat in the audience. I try to find a free seat that is as far away from Beth as possible but the only ones that are free are near her, so I sit by her. Beth has done her eye makeup extra dark today so she looks like a woman instead of a fucking schoolgirl. This aggravates me. I imagine Matt seeing her like that. I fantasize about Beth accidently getting pregnant by Matt and having to fall off the face of the earth. I make myself think about my nonexistent acting career and all the obstacles I'll have to face. This is the only thing that makes me feel worse than seeing Beth. At least it gets my mind off her.

It is the evening of the first round of showcase auditions and I've totally procrastinated because of fear and nervousness. I never procrastinate doing my scenes for school. I've been meaning to check my calendar, but I've avoided it due to dread and anxiety. Plus I don't know where my calendar is; probably buried under one of the stacks of papers in the mess that is my room. I've also written down to work on the audition piece on one of the many to-do lists I have but rarely look at because they are too overwhelming.

I don't want to go. I'm not prepared. If I was prepared I'd be less anxious but I decide to make myself go anyway. I don't even have the stupid monologue memorized, let alone rehearsed.

I look over it and the thoughts and ideas in it as a step towards rehearsing it. I know what choice I'll use in the monologue but I don't know if it will still work because I haven't used it in a while. Matt is my choice and I think I might be over him by now and won't be able to make the choice personal.

I change my clothes for the audition but I have nothing to wear as usual. I drive to school. It is raining. Rain usually inspires me but now it is just a hassle and making everything harder. I can't enjoy it. It doesn't relax me. School doesn't feel the same today. It feels like a scary place instead of a home away from home, or my acting sanctuary safe place where my true talent can rise up with all the talented, capable teachers around me, especially Rourke.

I do the audition. I suck.

On Monday Penn and I are about to start rehearsing. It is late at night. We are going to perform the scene for the third time in class, six days from now, and I am starting to freak out about it.

I am already upset and pissy about what had happened earlier in the day. I can't believe my other scene partner; said she was *tired*. I can't believe that *tired* was her biggest goddamn problem. She said she couldn't get to class 'cause her car broke down. I'd been enraged and thought it was a lie or some lame excuse and she just didn't want to come. We missed our time slot because of her. She wasted my time, money and all I invested. I was all prepared and had contained my stress, nerves and sat through all that and now we weren't even doing the scene. It will take longer for me to learn to act if I ever learn, because she is a flakey bitch who fucked me over.

Anyway, in rehearsal Penn and I start improvising. I sit in one of the chairs off stage. Penn is sitting on the stage leaning against a wall. He's taken his shirt off. He is examining his stomach and trying to grab his nonexistent fat rolls again. I assume he is trying to get into his role by doing this, playing the disheveled and depressed Dustin.

"Look at me," he says.

"Yeah I know. You're getting fat." He isn't fat at all. In fact, I like how he looks.

"Don't wear that shirt again," Penn says.

The asshole side of him goes on to talk about the color of my shirt. He suggests I wear light purple. I don't know who he thinks he is. That is very rude of him. Now I feel so embarrassed and that I should spend more time picking out my outfits. But almost every other shirt I tried on was too tight in the stomach and it showed how bloated I looked. So I chose one of the looser ones I had, but it wasn't that cute, and definitely not sexy.

I get up and go to the window. I am turned away from him.

"I love your ass," Penn says.

I wear my favorite pair of jeans. They are old and very faded in the butt. I turn around to look at him.

"I can't believe you don't like to be touched. I find it so intriguing. I just wanna grab you." He makes a grabbing gesture with his hands.

I want him to grab me too. I have thought saying I don't like to be touched might throw him, and I am right because he keeps bringing it up. And he uses the word *intriguing* instead of *interesting* just like Rourke always does; it is cute.

"You're just saying that for the scene. You've never hit

on me. You're not hitting on me," I say trying to sound angry instead of flattered.

"You wouldn't know it if I was," he says.

I am actually angry now. I don't know what to say or even what to think. How does he know that? How does he always just know things? How does he know I'm not very experienced? It's not like I have a sign on my forehead. It may have been totally true in the past but I am maturing fast in a lot of areas because of acting, needing to wise up for playing different sides of me and different types of scenes. Still, I hate he knows how naive I am and wish he and other people thought I was a big slut. This is the same theme that we've improvised before. Another thing I don't "understand" and something Penn apparently does.

"Is that why you like Roxanne?" I say.

Penn always gives such a knowing personal inflection when he says the line about my character Stacy not "understanding." I'm not happy about this, and the fact he doesn't like things about me, except I don't know for sure what. He always seems to take it so personal that I can't "understand." It seems like the thing he despises and hates most, but why the hell does he always have to rub it in my face?

When we perform for the third time in class the scene goes okay. The only thing I really need to talk to Rourke about is how to make it more personal. Rourke tells me to repeat what I did, acting-wise, and do the scene again.

We are rehearsing in one of the classrooms at school and this is our second–to–last rehearsal before Penn leaves. I sit in one of the awkward old chairs, trying to hold my stomach in. My hair is up. I had gotten up so early this morning to exercise and then rushed getting ready to be on time for work, that I hadn't had time to wash it. I don't like how it looks and feel uncomfortable when it isn't perfectly freshly washed. So I wear it up. Put it up neatly though because I knew I'd be seeing Penn.

"Why do you always wear your hair up?" Penn asks.

He is wrong because I don't always wear it up. I usually only like wearing it down when I've straightened it and it looks good. My impulse is to put my hair down. So I do even though I don't want him to see me such a mess. I don't want to say it hasn't been down because I haven't washed it.

Anna has stick perfectly straight, high-volume, shinny hair.

I think we shouldn't be doing so much improvisation but Rourke said to. Even though we have created the attraction and relationship, he wants us to make it more personal.

"Fine, oh, so you can't stand to look at me with my hair up, like I have to always look like I walked off the cover of *Maxim* just so you'll shut up," I say.

He smiles. "I'm gonna miss your mood."

Why does he have to say things like that? I just want to hold him, but I think it isn't right for the scene. In the scene Dustin and Stacy are probably in love. At least those types of feelings are there but Stacy is furious with him for almost the entire scene. And why can't Penn just yell back like a normal person?

He goes on. "I like your hair down."

It is good I like him, but not when I am trying to create the opening of the scene and he is taking the wind out of my anger. How can I possible be mad at him when he is being so adorable? When I want to laugh and talk with him all day and not do the scene? But a part of Stacy wants that too so it is okay, I think. Working with Penn and this scene is even more confusing then I usually get working on a scene. When he is being nice I feel like I forget about all the bad things about him. It is so hard.

I get up and walk on stage. I move the clasp on the

necklace I am wearing. It has sunk down to where the charm is. It used to have two charms on it that were my initials, but since the "B" charm broke off, it just has a "D" now for my last name, Dallago. I still wear it because I love it. Penn notices me straightening it on my neck.

"D for 'don't touch,'" he says.

"Funny," I say, not sounding amused at all. "It's for Dallago," I finish.

"I'm leaving in less than a week. Are you gonna miss me?" Penn asks for what now seems like the tenth time.

I had kept saying no, but now he brings it up, yet again. I sit cross-legged on stage and can see my legs covered in jeans. I look at the floor.

"I'll miss you more than you'll know," I say. My face feels warm. I look at him. I'm not sure what to do next. I feel the words I said came out sounding very high-pitched and maybe too young.

"I'll miss you too," Penn says gently. He looks right at me.

"What will you miss?" I ask.

"I'll miss your mood. And your bright sunshine smile and your never-sarcastic remarks."

I grab a piece of my hair and start running it through my fingers.

"I like when you do that with your hair," Penn says. He has noticed again.

Maybe he is my best friend and he is going to leave. I want to tell him things, tell him more but I stop myself. Penn doesn't only talk about girls. He talks about acting and how he used to want to be The Karate Kid. I don't say anything but that's why I got into acting too. I originally wanted to be Heather Rolland in the TV show *Gold*. She was gorgeous and strong. In every episode she would go on a     secret     mission     and     save     the     world.

# 8.  A RIVER RUNS THROUGH IT

It is Saturday and my last rehearsal with Penn. In three days we will be performing for the fourth and last time in class on Tuesday. Next week is the end of the semester and Penn will be leaving for his flight back to Switzerland that day after class. He asked me a couple weeks ago if I could give him a ride to the airport and I said yes.

I arrive at Penn's. He has finally shaved and I can see his face again, probably because he'd visited a relative the day before.

"I have to be brilliant by tomorrow," I say.

"Why do you always have to be brilliant?"

I don't understand his question at all. Why would anyone want to be less than brilliant? Maybe I don't have to be brilliant, but I want to make a giant leap in how much I learn.

"Two other people offered me rides to the airport so you don't have to take me if it's too much trouble. I can get a ride from one of them," Penn says.

"No, I wanna take you." I do want to and he'd asked me first anyway.

We improvise the same scene we've been doing for three months for thirty minutes in Penn's room. It's the point where Stacy barges into Dustin's house, pissed. After Dustin broke up with Stacy, he starting dating her cousin, and she felt stabbed in the back, again. Penn's shirt is off and he is wearing cutoff sweatpants he claims he went running in, and then didn't wash.

### Blake as Stacy:
### "What's happened between you two?"

*Can I ever really trust you Penn?*

### Penn as Dustin:
### "I don't know why you're asking? But still, we never talk about you."

Penn is eating M&Ms while picking at one of his toenails, pretending to be gross again. Since he's poured out all the M&Ms onto the carpet, he is eating them off the floor.

### Blake as Stacy:
### "I want you to swear to me you won't go near her again."

*Stop hurting me Penn.*

I walk around his room and look at the mess on the floor. His new guitar is in the corner. I pick up and hesitantly smell the glass of milk he'd offered me earlier in the scene and I'd refused to drink.

### Penn as Dustin:

### "I don't get why this matters to you. I thought you didn't care about me anymore."

On the floor are crumpled up papers, wrinkled clothes and a *Hustler* magazine. I know Penn had bought it as a prop for an improv he did with his other scene partner, Niles, at school. So why hasn't he thrown it away yet? Penn, the bastard, just happened to leave it because he knew it would bother me. I've never seen a magazine like that before. I pick it up and flip through a few pages. One photo spread is of a naked girl standing on the beach. Her back faces the camera and her head is turned back smiling at the lens. Her entire backside is in the shot including her butt.

I suddenly feel very fat and pale and throw the magazine down in disgust.

### Blake as Stacy:
### "This isn't just some girl. I'm related to her."

I look at my notes written next to the scripted page. *I need you Penn, and you know we have something special, so how could you talk about girls in such a shitty way when you're around me?*

Penn tears off a piece of toenail and drops it on the carpet. He does it to annoy me because he waits until I am looking at him to drop it. Good thing my shoes are on. Penn's aren't. I hate myself for being attracted to someone I am disgusted by.

### Penn as Dustin:
### "No, you're asking because you're still attached to me."

### Blake as Stacy:
### "Was attached."

*I hate you Penn.*

### Penn as Dustin:
### "You haven't stopped loving me. What are you doing every day without me?"

Penn puts on his faded black T-shirt that has been lying on the floor.

### Blake as Stacy:
### "I've been getting by. I'm in pain because of you. If I still love you I also hate you more. I never imagined you would do this. I don't know what's happened to you. You twist everything around. I thought what you felt for me was love."

I look down at my script. My note written next to the last line is *I miss you.* I put the glass of milk down that I've been holding and put one hand in my jeans pocket. *Don't leave me Penn.*

### Penn as Dustin:
### "It was. It is."

Penn moves closer to me and reaches for my hand. I push his arm away and walk to the other side of the room.

### Blake as Stacy:
### "Then why would you ruin everything for me?"

I think and feel *you destroyed me and fuck you* as I say my line. I think this about Penn, but at this point he and Dustin are becoming interchangeable.

Penn remains standing at the other side of the room. He crouches down to pick up a brown M&M.

### Penn as Dustin:
### "Do you think my life is so great and everything is under

**control for me? It's not. I'm a mess and I'm messed up in my mind a lot. I told you this already. I'm just trying to get things to make sense. But I love you, I want you."**

*I believe every word, vowel and sound he says to me.*

It is hard to remember and know who I am. Am I really Stacy or Blake?

I stand in front of the closed door in his room. Penn comes over to me again and reaches for my hand. I let him take it. We had done this part of the scene our first rehearsal and many other times since. It felt a little strange saying the words the first time. It is different now. This is the best part of acting when it feels so real; I don't even feel like I am acting.

### Blake as Stacy:
### "I'm afraid."

I have a thought written down next to this line on the script, but I don't use it because I am experiencing the exact thing as Stacy, except more. *I'm afraid—to let someone in. To let you know the real me, to feel so much for you, to be so intimate even though it's only with words.*

I still hesitantly hold Penn's hand. Penn's thumb strokes my hand. His other palm rests on my side above my hip.

### Penn as Dustin:
### "I am too but this is what I want. I can't stop."

This is the last line of the scene. We are done, but I always feel really self-conscious when it is over, so I laugh, push his hand off me and walk away from him.

Penn has a glint in his eye. "It says here 'they kiss passionately,'" Penn says, referring to the script.

"Let's do the scene one more time. Then I should go. I have to get up really early."

Tuesday we do our scene for the last time for Rourke. It actually goes pretty well for me. Rourke thinks the scene is strong and there is only a small thing I have to work on. He thinks my part is moving and impacting. He says he sees me as Stacy, that I made my lines real and a lot of other things.

In acting, what he said are all very good things but I can't help thinking about the one thing I did wrong. It brings me down and eats at me. Penn doesn't get as good a critique as me but nothing usually gets him down. He takes things in their accurate perspective.

After the scene, Penn goes to sit on the floor in the back of class. I usually like to sit in the chairs, but I sit next to him on the floor and hold onto his arm because it feels natural and I only have two more hours with him. We watch the next scene that goes up. Then he wanders off at the class break to say goodbye to people and run last-minute errands. Shouldn't he have already done that? I am going to stay until class is over and then meet him at his friend's house where he'd stayed the night before. He'd stayed there because it is walking distance to school. He's already sold his motorcycle. He sent me a text message the day he sold it that said, *It's sold. Could've been cool going for a final ride on Mulholland...*

After class I drive the two blocks to his friend's house. Penn meets me outside and puts money in the parking meter before I even have a chance to think about it. I follow him down the hall to the apartment he is staying in. I want to talk to him now but we are rushed. Since the scene is finally done, I can finally talk to him for real, can finally get the truth from him. Except now I have only about thirty minutes. I always seem to be in a rush as if there isn't very much time. My workaholism on the scene distracted me from the fact that he is actually leaving. God, why do we have to be rushing again?

We get to the apartment. His *friend* is a girl. Her name is

Anita and we immediately recognize each other because she used to go to Strasberg. Was that one of the girls he said he had sex with? It hurts my mind trying to figure him out. I never really thought much of Anita who I knew from a few semesters ago at school but now I hate her and the slutty dress she is wearing. She is on her way out. Penn hugs her goodbye and she leaves.

"I have to take a shower," Penn says.

"What?" I look at the clock.

"I still haven't taken a shower."

"I'm worried you're going to miss your flight."

"Me too," he replies.

Like that is comforting.

"It's going to be the fastest shower ever," and he disappears into the bathroom.

I sit on the couch and watch him rush to get ready. I realize he isn't even done packing when I notice him gathering things from around the apartment and adding them to his luggage.

Finally on the road, Penn is on my phone asking for advice about what is the fastest way to get to the airport. I am glad he is figuring out a quick way to get there because we are cutting it really close and I suck at directions.

He hangs up the phone. I turn onto La Cienega. We are on our way.

"Why can't you stay longer?" I ask.

"I've been here eighty-nine days and I can only stay for ninety."

"Oh God."

"I'm on a tourist visa."

"Oh."

Now is the time I can say all I want to say and be honest and it won't affect the scene, but my mind is blank. I don't know where to start. I just feel stressed out or stupid for building up the moment. I keep looking over at Penn. He is tired. Really tired because he keeps yawning and he has pushed his seat far back. He lounges but he still talks enthusiastically as he talks about a scene he did the night before.

I interrupt his monologue about the scene. "Um, I feel like I can finally talk to you for real 'cause the scene is over," I say. Fuck. That came out lame. But it was all I could manage to say.

"We always talk real," Penn says.

Then he continues talking about his scene. I rack my brain again thinking about what to say, how to say it, when to say it and in what way. I am getting very anxious and start not to even hear Penn. As we get closer to the airport I start to freak out even more. Maybe I am just putting too much pressure on myself. Maybe I should just not say anything. I decide that. I spend most of the ride in silence listening to him talk about his scene and sometimes asking about it, while thinking I'm using up all my moments to say what I really want. Before I know it, I see the on-ramps for the airport terminals. It is now. I have waited long enough.

I should ask if he is going back to live with his girlfriend, if he has a girlfriend. I still am not sure. The time is now to tell him how much he means to me, but I continue driving, silent.

I pull up to the airport curb. We made it just in time. I get out with Penn and help him get his bags out of the car. It is still light out. I notice the airport security guard on the curb. Penn goes over to ask the guy where to check in. He walks back over to me to say goodbye.

"You have to keep in touch," I say.

"I thought you didn't wanna be friends."

"I changed my mind I want us to be friends."

"I'll keep in touch," he says.

"You promise."

"I promise."

I feel nervous and don't know what else to say. My body feels very stiff and like I forget how to stand normal. I cross my hands over my chest. He touches my forearms, pulls them apart and hugs me. We kiss each other on the cheeks.

"I don't want you to go," I whine.

"I'll be back but I don't know when yet."

He takes my hands and holds them for a second. He squeezes them. I squeeze back.

"I have to go," Penn says.

"Kay."

He gives me a slight closed mouth smile as he walks away. The automatic doors open and he goes inside. I see another car has its blinker on, urging me to move my car. They want my spot. I get in, turn on the engine and drive away. I didn't get any of the "truth" I planned. But maybe I feel the truth and the rest doesn't really seem to matter anymore.

The next day at school the air is empty and stale. What is the point? I won't see him anymore, practically skipping in with a smile on his face.

"Have you talked to him?" George asks.

I pretend I don't know who "him" is. It is weird being so upset. And if I talk about it I'll look weak or something. Or like the girl left behind or like I get too involved with my coworkers. I wish I wasn't fazed.

# PART 2

# 9.  CRUEL INTENTIONS

It's Thursday. Penn left two days ago. It's good that it's a very busy time for me. In fact, it's good he left. I can concentrate better on other stuff I have to do. It's great he left. We got to perform *Forgotten Minds* many times in class in just one semester and that was important. I don't feel sad because I didn't really care about him. It is just the scene I cared about.

I find myself suddenly very hungry. I've been anxious from the second I woke up this morning and could not eat. Usually I try to eat very small meals every two hours. Today I did not do this. I did eat some breakfast, soy milk and protein cereal.

It's 6 p.m. and I'm done with school for the day. I don't want to go home to eat because there's nothing in the fridge. I decide to order pizza. I order two large pizzas and two boxes of cinnamon sticks. Pizza is my favorite food of all time but I eat it rarely because it's not good for me. But when I do eat it I tend to eat a lot because it's so good.

I pick up the pizza from Pizza Hut and get in the car with it. The smell takes over the car, the commercialized cheese and preservatives. For some reason I feel guilty, like I'm committing a crime. I don't want anyone to see me with it. It comes in neat boxes and is cut evenly, probably by a machine. The pizza is just the size of the boxes given to me. I am a rebel. I should not eat this pizza. It's wrong. It's evil. This is cheap, cancer-causing, cellulite-producing, artery-clogging food. Yet I rebel. I want it so bad and don't understand why people who eat whatever they want wouldn't eat this all the time, every day.

I eat the pizza. It tastes like heaven. I watch *The Sopranos*.

I eat more. The first pizza's gone. I don't feel full or even slightly full.

I eat the cinnamon sticks. I love their texture in my mouth, warm and soft. I eat almost both boxes of the dessert. There is one stick left and no frosting. I want to eat the last stick, but can't, can't because I now feel sick. My stomach hurts and my mouth is cut up from the pizza and the crust.

I zone out to *The Sopranos*. Tony is very angry. I love *The Sopranos* for a lot of reasons. One is because Tony always says whatever he wants. He doesn't censor himself. Well, not usually. He also does whatever he wants, and sleeps with whoever he wants. In certain ways, I wish I could be more like that. An hour passes. I get up to put the cinnamon sticks box in the fridge. It's an effort as my stomach hurts and I feel like I caught the flu. I should put the leftover pizza in the fridge too but can't. I can't look at it because it makes me feel even sicker when I look at it. I feel it in my throat. I take the pizza box and throw it away in the dumpster outside my apartment, throwing away the untouched whole pizza inside it. It's good I threw it away as I'll never be able to eat pizza again, and will never want it again and will never even crave it again. Just the thought of it disgusts me.

I lie down in bed and fall asleep by 8:30 p.m.

The next morning I rush to the gym at 6 a.m. and make sure to do a really good workout. I stay for two hours and thirty minutes to get back on track with my food, and to make up for how many calories I ate. I didn't eat breakfast as the sight of food now makes my stomach turn. It doesn't matter because I went to the gym with the food still in my stomach from last night.

When I say a hard workout, I do mean hard. It's okay to eat pizza because I exercise. My workout plan is typed in a binder I take to the gym. It's not a day I have morning classes. When it is, I go at 5 a.m. I go in the morning because I have the most energy and can get the best workout. Also, I like to go as early as possible because after I do resistance training and cardio my metabolism is sped up. So there are more hours to have a faster metabolism than if I went at night. In the end, morning training burns more calories and fat, so the earlier I go, the more time my body has to work off and digest correctly what I ate. I go to bed early to get enough rest to do conditioning and weight-lifting.

I switch between a five-day body split and some days I work my whole body. I've never gone longer than four days in a row without training. If I go on vacation, than I do exercises in my hotel room. I used to not work out when sick or injured but now try to do calf raises, pistol squats, et cetera, and cardio as much as I can. I need to do extra-great routines every day to burn off the times when I eat a lot. I also work out as much as possible so I can eat sweets sometimes.

Exercise is always a priority. I don't understand when people say they don't have time. I plan my day, appointments, rehearsal, socializing, work, all around when I'll go to the gym. I make time, and if I don't have time I sleep less and wake up earlier in the morning. Anyway, exercise is supposed to give you energy. I still go even if I'm tired; I'd just push myself more. I'm tougher than they are. At the gym I count the number of sets and reps I do. It's always exactly even. For step-ups I use 20-pound dumbbells and do five sets of 20, but lately I've been doing more, 12 to 15 sets because I'm worried about my bloated stomach and that my body fat percentage is up. My goal's still to be at 13 percent or lower. Sometimes I tell myself I have worked out enough for one day, but then feel I have a little more in me so I'll do another set, and then another. If I feel I miscounted a set or rep, I always do extra.

Before leaving home I have to make sure my iPod's charged, and that I have a sweatshirt, water, towel, and the right clothes on. All of this keeps me focused to push myself more. Sometimes I prepare the night before so nothing stops me in the morning.

I check my email.

Normally I never check it. It gives me anxiety and I hate feeling obligated to write people back. This time I check it excitedly to see if Penn wrote. He hasn't. I don't have his phone number in Switzerland, only his L.A. number. His L.A. number was a contracted cell phone. He bought minutes on it. It was temporary, just like him. His phone ran out of minutes before he left. That's why I lent him my cell phone so he could get directions from his friend while we were on the way to the airport.

I hate Penn. Hate him for not writing to me and not thinking about me. But it doesn't matter. I don't have time for men, or even people, and have enough problems trying to be a successful actress.

Three weeks later I do a scene in Rourke's class. It's a very difficult scene. I rehearsed it to perfection. The scene goes great. Rourke says my talent and technique are developing even more; that all my hard work is paying off. And it's very rare that he sees as much change and growth in an actor that he sees in me. It's what I've been hoping to hear from him for two years, but I don't care. I feel like shit. Not happy or relieved. I'm bored with acting and bored with school. I probably shouldn't be an actress anyway. It was a stupid idea. Normally Rourke is mean to the core, and I'm sick of dealing with him, of tiptoeing around him and his temper, and having to live up to his impossible standards.

At home, my apartment is a goddamn mess and I don't want to clean it. I don't care if my jeans are ironed at the creases anymore. I throw them on the floor instead of folding them. It doesn't matter if they get dusty. I stop straightening my hair.

I go to the gym more, because this is what matters. I haven't had an appetite lately. This is awesome. I like how my body looks like this. I don't have to worry about food that much, about eating healthy and right. When I measure my body fat percentage in a month, it might be lower than ever.

I still rehearse. I'm a machine at rehearsing. Nothing stops me. I rehearse after work until 3 a.m. I don't go outside. I don't like the sun and it's too hot. Plus, I have too much to do. I drink coffee before I go to the gym now. It helps my workouts. I don't see Ashley much. I'm always at the gym before she wakes up, and when I come home she's already at work.

I still don't have much of an appetite so I milk the situation by buying low-fat, low-carb, no-sugar, high-protein foods. It's almost easy now to eat this way. I don't want any other food or really any food at all. Before my stomach starts to hurt and growl, I shove some food down my throat and make myself swallow it without really chewing. I don't want to taste it. My stomach seems flatter than normal when I put on jeans and when I look in the mirror. I like this.

I see Beth at school. She is a hundred percent superficial, the shallowest person I have ever met, and she's always smiling. She wears a navy blue dress today. It looks stupid. She comes up to talk to me.

We exchange small talk. This leads her into telling me that she gets restless in Rourke's class. So she can't help but text on her iPhone when she's sitting in the audience.

I still hate Beth, her insides and her outside. She is the epitome of shallow, empty, cheap slapstick comedies, a slap in the face. She is a package, only a shiny outside that can memorize a line the same way a chimpanzee can. She is forgotten. Not an actor. She's an animated cartoon. She doesn't understand struggle or the depth of experiences people have.

I wanna tell her all this and tell her she breaks my heart. That she breaks my heart into a million pieces every time I see her. Acting is being private in public. That's what I'm taught. Beth doesn't even really get nervous. I heard her tell Rourke that. I get very nervous and scared. Learning the technique of acting is the hardest thing I've ever done and I do it for those moments on screen I'll never forget. I expose my private hell or heaven to the audience. Beth degrades what movies and acting are. Most of the time characters demonstrate the struggles in life, the hard times, not the glamorous times; the fancy dresses and perfect hair times. Characters show the moments when they're a mess and in the trenches. That's that beautiful part, because Beth doesn't try to build these kinds of true experiences in her acting, I'm torn apart. She will not, never has and never will say something from her heart like what real actors do.

She will never be the actress I watched on the screen when I was ten. I saw the way she looked at a man with love, desire, heartache and fear, when she let him comfort her because she had never been comforted before in her life. At the time, I was moved and cried. In fact I didn't even want to watch it because it made me so sad but couldn't stop watching because it was so good.

Beth doesn't have any freckles. She doesn't think like me and never will. She doesn't care, doesn't care either way, if she gives meaningful performances or empty ones. She isn't an actor. She is a model who talks but shouldn't be allowed to talk.

It's Tuesday, but I didn't dress up today. In fact, I didn't even put on fucking mascara. I look like shit. Beth looks perfect. Her dress is new. I can tell because it looks like it hasn't been washed yet. I feel thin but am wearing a baggy sweatshirt. Still, it hangs nicely on my shoulders. I want to say every crude thing, the crudest things I can think of, to her. So crude that they hurt me, but I don't.

I lie to her now. I tell her I like her phone case and I'm thinking about getting one. Hell, I even ask where she got it.

She answers me, not suspecting a thing. She's a moron.

I walk away. She's exhausting, although maybe I'm not exhausted. Maybe I'm fed up, not even with Beth but with myself.


My room's a mess. I want to clean it but need to train first. I have a list of things I must get done today, like most days. There are clothes covering the floor. Open containers of food. Papers and receipts are in a big stack on the carpet because my desk and dresser are covered with crap already, but all that I can feel is how huge I am and know I'm not skinny.

I've gained weight since I last saw Beth, so I change to go workout. I dress for the gym in baggy clothes, trying to cover my body and worrying how humiliated I am when people see me. I put on a thong and black stretch pants. I was going to put my shoes on and leave but notice there's the indent in my pants where the sides and back of my underwear are pushing into my skin. They're doing this because my body is so chubby. I can't leave the house this way.

I change into a bigger pair of underwear so there will be less noticeable indents. My feet hurt. I look down to see what it is. My toenails are too long and are cutting into the sides of my toes. I was on my feet a lot yesterday doing cardio, eighty minutes. But I can't cut them. It will take too long to cut and file them. I've got to get to the gym. I have this fear something will get in the way of me exercising. That I'll get lazy or overwhelmed with something else. I know I'll feel better when I'm doing something to lose weight. I'll just ignore the pain and cut my toenails later. I was going to check the pain in my feet last night, but without meaning to I fell asleep.

I do cardio after weights because this preserves more of my lean muscle mass and burns the most fat. But I'm not sure why I'm worrying about this detail. I should focus on burning the most calories. I start warming up with box jumps but feel the food in my stomach from the night before and how tight it feels. I will have to do double what I normally do and work twice as hard today.

I start working out my lower body with lunges. I do walking lunges and reverse lunges. I don't just do any exercises. Reverse lunges and walking lunges are both superior to regular lunges. My stabilizing muscles are more involved in walking lunges, and in reverse lunges my posterior chain is further engaged. So they sculpt my body the way I want. I do squats. I used to wait between sets but now do shoulder raises in between. I think about the muscle I'm exercising as I'm working it and look at my body in the mirror to make sure my technique is right.

At the gym, I impulsively watch the cooking channel on the TV attached to the elliptical. I turn on the show because I'm hungry. Even though I just ate, ate enough I should feel full. I know I can't really eat more, but I do want to look at food. I'm trying to lose weight and lower my body fat percentage. It all looks so good. Down to the color and the way it's displayed and prepared. It's hard to eat less because I think about food so much. I like to see the food because if I can't eat it, I at least want to look at it. It helps me stay sustained. It's a trick I learned. I'm doing more and more of these secret tricks. In the past I used to do weight training to tone and shape my body. To keep my body composition, which is a combination of body fat percentage and lean muscle mass, where I wanted it and so I would stay thin. Now I do it mainly to burn calories.

I do as many sets and reps as I can in the time I have and as many two-minute sets of planks as I can. There are tons of gym towels in my car. I've started to bring bigger and bigger towels because I can't stop sweating. The towels get soaked with sweat. I still use them because no towel is big enough. Something is off today because I feel so hot while doing my routine. I can't get cool, not even after pouring water on my T-shirt and hair. It's been really hot this week, and the air conditioning was broken earlier in the week. They say it's been fixed, but I go and ask the desk lady to be sure.

"It's on, it's been on all day," she says and looks at me like I'm crazy.

She must have been getting complaints from other members about the heat, so her answer and expression make no sense to me.

It's nighttime. I'm worried and anxious I will go hungry. Anxious about tomorrow morning, that I'll have nothing to eat and will be starving the second I wake up. So I need to prepare and go to the grocery store. I feel like my over-the-top stress of feeling starved is slightly odd.

I'm sure to buy plenty of breakfast food at the store.

At home I begin my preparations. Line up what I'll eat. Make sure there are clean utensils to use and that a place is clear on my table to eat. My routine is always the same. I wake up, brush my teeth and then go to the kitchen. I prepare my bagel for tomorrow. Put one bagel in a ziploc bag in front of the toaster because I think it will be faster to eat that way. Things have completely changed this month. Instead of having no appetite, I'm hungry all the time, and all I can think about is food.

The next morning I walk to the kitchen. I see the bagel. I'm too hungry to wait for it to toast. So I don't toast it. I eat it with cream cheese. Eat the tub of cream cheese I bought, all of Ashley's cream cheese and eight bagels. I'm disgusting. I can't even throw it up. I tried that last weekend and it didn't work. Even looked up on the Internet how to do it, and that didn't work either. My throat still hurts from the toothbrush I shoved down it. I rush to the grocery store and buy cream cheese to put back in the fridge, the same brand Ashley had so she won't know I ate hers.

Rehearsal is in an hour. I have to get ready. My plan to go to the gym went to shit since now there's no time. I spent too much time eating. In my room there're piles of papers on the floor and clothes covering the carpet. I don't even step over them, just step on them now. I go to my closet and look for my baggiest shirt and my hat. I'll have to take the hat off for rehearsal but can wear it before I get there. I should have eaten something else. If only I found the exact food to satisfy my craving, then I'd finally feel full. I put on the shirt. It's not baggy enough. It shows how fat I am, how much weight I've gained. I wear old, stretched out leggings because none of my size-four jeans fit me, they hurt. Putting on my riding boots makes all the calluses I have from running hurt. So does zipping them. They feel uncomfortably tight on my calves. It's hard to get them to zip. I'm an elephant. My legs rub together in a different, awful way than they used to. A headache pounds on the left side of my head.

I walk into school and up the stairs to the room where we'll be rehearsing. I feel dizzy and stuffed. I will never eat that much again. I'll never do it again. That was the last time. I just won't eat for a week. Yes, that's what I'll do. That will make up for the calories I ate, and I'll stick to my diet to lose three pounds a week.

My scene partner isn't here yet. I get out my calendar and mark the number of days it will take me to lose the weight I've just gained. I use the calculator on my phone. Twenty days if I eat two hundred calories a day. No, that's too many. If I don't eat anything, then I will be back on track in nine days. That's better. I will be thin and fine in nine days. That's a lot better.

I'm upset. It will be hell to not eat for nine days. I'm already hungry and already want to eat. Nine days is too long. If I exercise twice a day with almost no calorie intake then I can be back to my old weight in only six days. That's good. I can do six days, and it's less than a week. I mark my calendar. I do it in code so no one knows what it means.

It's three weeks later. I have lost the weight. I lost it in seven days. Why don't I feel right? Slightly energized or slightly happy? I don't know. It's a mystery. Once I am paying for everything myself, then I won't feel anxious. In my room I look at my face in the mirror and can't stand the sight of it. I try on my tightest pair of jeans, a small size four. They fit. They haven't fit for three months. Penn has been gone three months. I wore these jeans the day he left because I wanted to look beautiful for him. But my body doesn't seem the same as before, probably because my body fat percentage is higher and I look worse. I change my pants and clean my room.

I'm fine now. I'm getting my hair cut tomorrow. I will feel better then, and my room is clean now. I will just try harder and things will be better.

# 10. THE HUNGER GAMES

I get my hair cut then go to school. It's 6 p.m. I eat something. It's 6:30 p.m. I've already been to the gym. Should I go again and run because I feel angry and it might be therapeutic? Instead, I decide to run an errand.

I see a guy in my aisle at Target. He walks by me. Oh yeah, I'm supposed to check him out because this is "the new me." I look back at him — well, back at his shoes. They're ugly. I leave.

I don't really remember Penn being here. It seems like three lifetimes ago. It does. I don't miss Penn today. I haven't really missed him at all since he left. But if I did, I'd miss his blue eyes and the way he looked at me. We have written back and fourth to each other in some emails.

At home, in my bedroom, I'm lying on my bed too tired to move. I worked out for five hours today, yesterday for six hours. I was lazy today. My sports bra squeezes around my chest; it's too small. It's still wet from sweat, along with the rest of my clothes, and it's making indents in my skin. But I'm too tired to get up and walk across the room to change. My head itches, maybe from being cold with sweat. My lips feel very dry. Dry to the point where they're stinging but I don't have energy to get up to find Vaseline or ChapStick. I lick my lips but it doesn't help the stinging. The sweat dried on them tastes salty as well as the edges around my mouth. My feet are elevated on two long pillows. My shins and feet constantly ache, so I've come into a routine where I elevate them every night before bed and fall asleep like that so they stay high up all night. But sometimes my shins hurt so bad that the pain keeps me awake so I just lie awake most of the night. Today my feet hurt more than normal. Like earlier in the hallway my foot brushed my roommate Ashley's foot and I winced from the pain. She seemed confused as to what happened.

My calves and stomach feel swollen. I'm watching reruns of *The Sopranos* bootlegged on the computer. The streaming is so bad that the dialogue and scene starts and stops over and over like a broken record. It's four feet away from me but I'm not able to move that far to turn it off. My hands feel dry but they have stopped bleeding. There is some dried blood in the cracks of the skin on the top of my hands. They get so dry from all the gym chalk I use and from constantly sweating that they bleed even though I put lotion on them five times a day. No blood has gotten on my sheets.

"Can you turn that down?" Ashley yells from outside my closed door.

The broken record TV show is annoying her also. My socks squeeze and indent my skin too. I wore my thick and most comfortable ones today to the gym, trying to help my foot pain, but it didn't work and now it's backfiring. I want to sit up and take my socks off, but can't. Still lying down, I use my left foot to push down the top of my right sock and vise versa. It's a little better. I see the red indents of the socks on my ankles and calves. My bladder hurts. I've had to pee for an hour now but haven't been able to get up to walk to the bathroom either. I'll hold it a little longer. I drank three and a half gallons of water today because I read several places that if you drink a lot of water, you'll eat less and lose weight. I hope my eyes aren't swollen again when I wake up tomorrow like they have been for the last three weeks.

Most of my tongue is numb. I burnt it bad from eating something too hot this morning. I'm on this special diet and wanted to eat something sweet. So I cooked a pie in a recipe book of the diet. Couldn't just buy something from the store ready made to eat because that wouldn't be part of the diet. It had to be cooked for one hour at three hundred and fifty degrees, but I pulled it out of the oven fifteen minutes before the buzzer went off. Started eating it thirty seconds later because I was so hungry and couldn't stop myself. Half of the dough was still raw. I ate the whole pie within five minutes. My mouth felt like it was on fire and I worried about how bad it got burned. So I filled a large cup to the top full of ice and then filled the rest with water. I drank several cups of the freezing water hoping to make my mouth and my throat feel better. I also swished the water around my mouth to cool it that way.

"Did you hear me?" Ashley yells through the door over the sound of *The Sopranos*. She still wants me to turn off my laptop. But it is unplugged so eventually the battery will run out and the show will shut off.

Today I won't be able to exercise because I overslept and now have to go to the airport right after school to pick up Keri. She's visiting for the weekend. Keri and Ashley and I have been best friends since childhood. When we were little we'd play in the clover patch in Ashley's front yard looking for four-leaf clovers to get good luck. On St.

Patrick's Day, when we were a little older, we'd set out green food and then take it away, tricking Keri's little brother that there were leprechauns. That was back when things were different.

We are planning on going to the Beverly Center today, and then going out tonight 'cause that's what Keri wants and we want to show her a good time. Ashley's really excited to see Keri; me too. But I haven't kept in great touch so I feel guilty. Also I've been tired lately so I'm not sure I want to go shopping or out. Though I'm doing better then last week and am trying to cut back my exercise by twenty minutes a day because it was getting a little out of hand. I will just eat less instead and drink club soda to stay full.

Part of the reason I'm not one hundred percent excited about the weekend is because I had a crap day at school. At school I noticed Beth's bag because I thought it was pretty and real leather and expensive. She left it when she went to the other room to talk on her phone. For a second I thought about stealing it or tossing it in the smelly trash can with the remains of someone's overly mustard mushy sandwich that was in there. I mean, Beth didn't have something seriously wrong with her that made her feel tired all the time. Her face never got oily, even at the gym when I saw her with no makeup on.

After I pick up Keri from the airport we stop at the apartment to pick up Ashley and then head to the Beverly Center. We talk and shop. I window shop. But I'm not sure what's making me so sad about seeing my old friend. I am happy to see her, I am. But I don't react the way I thought I would when she tells me things that should make me happy. Instead, I get sad when Keri talks about her life in New York, and sadder when she talks about going out with her friends. Gloomy when she speaks about going to her normal job and her busy dating life. Empty when she talks about going out to eat. I can hardly think of anywhere I go out to eat. I never do anything but go to school, never live.

In the window of the Dior store I see the bag that was on Beth's arm today. But I didn't know it was Dior until I saw it on display. I'm not going to go in; it's not like I care and it's a snotty store anyway, but maybe if I lean real close to the window and crouch down then I can see the price tag. I tilt my head and see the tag is hanging by thin string and turned slightly sideways. So I get even closer to the window to wear my cheek almost touches it and see that it costs two thousand dollars.

A few hours later we're at a bar on Santa Monica Boulevard by my school. I notice my jeans are too big. The tight ones are too big and I can't make sense of this. I must have lost more weight. When I weighed myself it said so. Then why do I look bigger then ever when I look in the mirror? I can't comprehend this, or understand what I'm doing wrong trying to get my body back the way it used to be. Don't know what's going on or if I'm going completely insane. And, I mean, I'm not even drunk because I've only had one drink. I think things are going back to normal. I cleaned the kitchen today. I feel a little anxious but that could be from the nine cups of coffee I drank. I only drank them so I could wake up.

I didn't want to come out tonight. I had a bad day seeing Beth and also didn't get to audition for the second showcase round 'cause I didn't make it in. I found out today at school.

Ashley sits two vodka and soda drinks in front of me. She knows one of the bartenders so he gave her two for the price of one. I drink both drinks, one after another. I am really stressed and not feeling the alcohol yet so I ask Ashley to order another. At least then maybe this place can be tolerable. Is it because I ate too much today that I'm not feeling the drinks? But now that I think about it I don't think I ate anything today yet, but it's only 11:17 p.m. I look at my watch and wait for my next drink. Maybe I shouldn't have worn a watch to a bar. It makes me look too uptight. I do have fun bracelets on the same wrist with it, though.

There's a hangnail the size of Texas on my thumb. I feel it. It's really dry and hurts but I haven't been able to stop rubbing my finger on it all day. It makes the pain worse. How embarrassing. I wish I'd noticed it before I left, then I would have cut it. My nails are painted black because it's my favorite color and they look good that way. Heather Rolland in the TV show *Gold* always has black nails too.

It's an hour later. I've drunk three more drinks, but am still not relaxed, so I order another. This way I can have fun and behave like everyone else here. They all seem more relaxed and in the moment, including Ashley and Keri. There are a lot of calories in the alcohol but it's a special occasion and all. I just want to be normal. This is what those kinds of people seem to do. Plus I can just eat less tomorrow to make up for my high calorie intake today.

More time passes. I'm working on— actually I've lost count on how many vodka and sodas I've had so far, but anyway I'm working on my current one and feel very drunk. I order vodka and soda because I figure this will get me the most drunk with the least amount of calories. Plus I love club soda, except for the fact that it makes my stomach bloated.

"She's just such a bitch," I say to my drunk friends.

"God, I'd be embarrassed to carry such an expensive bag," Ashley says.

"I hate people who are born with everything. I bet she's miserable," Keri adds. It's good to have such nice friends. Maybe if I had all that money I wouldn't feel anxious, instead feeling safe. Or it would make up for all the things that suck in my life and then things would be balanced, and overall I'd feel better. I could cook less and have more time to do work and things would be easier. I would have the exact outfit that would make me feel comfortable while going on auditions. It's not that I'm superficial; I have my priorities straight. It's that the money represents power, opportunity and abundance. I am universally scraping by.

Ashley goes to flirt with some guys at the bar 'cause she is good at that kind of thing. Keri starts texting everyone she knows. I keep looking around the room and glancing at the door, hoping Matt won't show up. We'd gone here before and I know he likes it. Why had I come? But really, if I did run into him I probably wouldn't care. Keri and Ashley don't know about Matt or Penn. I mentioned this guy who was the most disciplined student I'd ever met, but that was all I said about Penn. One thing that's good is I finally don't care anymore if I run into Matt. With this realization, I am supposed to be happy

I leave the booth, wander outside and lean against the wall. Watch people drink beer on the porch. It's cold and I don't have a coat. I sit and slump down on the ice-cold concrete. Why isn't someone asking me what's wrong and consoling me now that I'm sad and drunk, alone outside a bar. Or a new extremely cute boy stranger is supposed to wonder up and hit on me. I would say no, but he would keep insisting and finally win me over. That's what happens in bad movies. At least something dramatic is supposed to happen. I figure I haven't drunk enough.

"Do you have a lighter?" some weird guy asks me.

I give him a dirty look. "No," I say, then go inside and back to the table.

I order another drink.

Ashley comes back to the table. She's wearing a big pink puffy scarf over a cool stringy tank. I drink my drink. I take the scarf off her and lie down on the booth and use the scarf as a blanket. The room's getting darker and louder, so loud I can't really make out what anybody's saying, and so dark that I can't really see anything either. Keri shoves her phone in my face. Tries to show me a text message I think. I squint trying to read it but still can't make out what it says. I curl up as much as I can on the booth.

"Blake sit up. That's dirty," Ashley says.

"Are you sleeping? Let's go," Keri says shaking me.

I sit up on the booth and then stand, praying I'll be able to walk to the car or walk at all. I hope we're headed back to the apartment because I know there's an unopened bottle of vodka there.

# 1. ONE FLEW OVER THE CUCKOO'S NEST

I'm being searched by a female police officer. I'm outside and the sun warms my face. I'm in what looks like a gated parking lot with a fence in front of me. The woman cop holds open a clear plastic bag in front of me. I'm not quite sure where I am; maybe the driveway of the police station? But I don't really try to think about it because my mind is gone. I just see some things around me but it's like I'm not really here. It's not even like I'm watching it on a movie. It's like a movie I saw a long time ago and it's just playing in the background.

"Please take off all your jewelry, your watch— everything— and what's in your pockets and place it in this bag," says the cop.

I do as I am told. She keeps talking, saying she will pat me down after my jewelry is off. I start to take off my jewelry, my mind still distorted and not sure what's going on. I hope I have the motor skills to undo the small clasps of my necklaces. I wear two necklaces, one long and one short. The long one is one I bought on the internet, the same one Heather Rolland always wears in *Gold*. The short one is my sterling silver "D" necklace. I take off my ring and the bracelets on both my wrists, as well as my watch. The woman cop holds open the bag and I place in my jewelry as I take off each piece.

I sit in the jail holding cell or whatever thing it is. This is where the woman cop escorted me. I just assume this as I don't remember how I got here. I don't feel much except for the diamond studs on the back of my jeans grinding into my butt. I'm sitting on a hard plastic ledge or seat and there is a cold wall behind me. Maybe concrete or brick, I'm not sure. I look at the door but it's a blur; is it locked? Could I just walk out and leave? I start replaying the scene in *Gold* where Joel confesses his love to Heather. It's my favorite scene. I replay exactly what the scene looked like and sounded like in my head, as well as try to find a comfortable way to sit on the concrete feeling seat. For a second I think I hear Rourke's voice outside the jail cell. I think I hear my mom's voice too. I replay another scene in my head I love from *Gold*.

I'm not sure if I have been waiting in the holding cell or whatever it is for around thirty minutes or four hours but now I'm going somewhere else. I don't recognize the shirt I am wearing. Maybe it's Ashley or Keri's?

I'm being transported by ambulance to somewhere else. I think to another facility. I told the two ambulance men that I could walk but they told me it's "policy" and so I had to be strapped to the gurney. The ride seems to take forever but the two ambulance men are nice and ask me what radio station I want to listen to. We finally arrive.

At the new place, the administration people or nurses –

I'm in too much of a daze to know who they are – tell me to wait. They say I have to talk to the doctor first and that he'll be here in twenty minutes.

When the doctor arrives I go into a private intake room with him. He's young and I can smell his expensive cologne. I start to sober up immediately except I haven't felt drunk, more like I'm dead and this is no longer my life. I'm just in a stupid video game or something. I become more in the present and less disoriented, realizing where I have been brought to: a metal institution. I realize these people, including the doctor I'm sitting in front of, want to make me stay here, meaning stay the night here.

I start to freak out at where I am and what's going on. This makes me feel a little more like myself, and even more like myself when I'm feeling humiliated and want to get out of this place as fast as possible. But with the alcohol finally breaking down in my body and brain, I remember things. Not nearly everything but probably why I'm in this place to begin with. After getting really out-of-my-mind drunk, I called my mother and told her I was suicidal. I think it was around 6:30 a.m., after drinking all night. She must have called the police so I wouldn't hurt myself. Because I also remember the woman cop saying "you're not in trouble" when she put me in handcuffs.

The doctor seems to read my mind. He reminds me of my phone call explaining why he can't release me from this hospital or locked ward.

"You told your mom you were suicidal," he says.

"I was just being dramatic and that's what happens when you get drunk. I don't feel that way at all now that I'm back in my right mind. I usually don't drink at all so when I had so much to drink last night it really messed me up," I plead.

"Do you need to have your stomach pumped?"

"No. I don't know. I haven't thrown up or anything but I feel really weird and out of it. I mean, I *did* feel that way.

Now I feel normal and happy. Like myself again."

The doctor looks down at a sheet of paper. Maybe it's my chart. He is very cold, odd and difficult to have a conversation with, like the way all doctors usually are.

"I left a message for your doctor listed here but I haven't heard back from him yet and your mother says you have a history of anxiety and depression," he says.

"Yeah, but that was way in the past. I don't want to stay here tonight but they said I have to talk to you before I can go. And that you have to approve to release me or something."

"No, I can't release you. I don't have all your background. How can I be sure that you won't act out after you just said you wanted to harm yourself? I'm putting you on a three-day hold. I'll re-evaluate your case on Monday, after I've heard from your primary doctor listed. You'll most likely be leaving on Tuesday," he announces.

He wears too much hair gel. And I don't like his I'm a young-rich-hot-shot-doctor attitude. I have the feeling he's just trying to get this meeting over with as fast as possible, so he can get back to his night life. That he's resentful in the first place for being called in on the weekend. I want to continue to explain myself and what happened, so he'll know I'm sane and let me leave, even if it takes hours, but I figure this is the end of the discussion.

The fog enters my mind again. The only thing I can think about is brushing my filthy teeth. I ask that nurse guy, staff worker or whatever the fuck he is for floss and a toothbrush. I've never gone without flossing every twenty four hours, ever. He says they don't have floss. They probably think people will try to strangle themselves or something with it. He brings me a toothbrush.

The man nurse shows me the room where I'll be spending the night and introduces me to my roommate, but he introduces me to her using my name and I feel violated, because I was planning to lie about my name and not talk to anyone here so it would never get known to the public I've ever been here. I talk to my roommate for a few minutes, mostly avoiding her questions in order to not reveal much about myself.

I go in the bathroom, lock the door and brush my teeth. Then I brush them again to make up for the no-floss rule or whatever. I am finishing scrubbing my gums with the so-called toothbrush which is actually a plastic thing with some bristles they *call* a toothbrush when my roommate knocks on the door.

"Are you done in there?" she asks.

If I was done why the fuck would I still be in here?

"No," I say swallowing a little toothpaste because that freaking bitch asked me a question and made me talk while I have a toothbrush in my mouth. A minute later I'm rinsing the toothpaste out of my mouth. I hear another knock.

"I need to come in. I think I'm going to throw up," my roommate says.

I quickly spit out the toothpaste water that has been sloshing around my mouth so I can answer and get a splash of gross toothpaste water on the side of my mouth.

"Why didn't you say anything?" I unlock the bathroom door and rush out.

My freak of a roommate rushes in gagging.

I leave the room to get away from that situation and to find some paper napkins to clean myself up with. I remember from our brief conversation she said she was in special-ed classes. I'm beginning to see why.

Thirty minutes later I finally feel clean after getting the bathroom to myself again or as clean as I can get without any of my stuff. Thank God it didn't smell of my roommate's vomit and there were no signs of her puke or weirdness. I contemplate whether to take a shower or not in this godforsaken place, then decided not to. This is a private hospital? That's what the man nurse had told me. God knows what a public hospital or mental institution looked like. Why couldn't I have just thrown up and then passed out like a normal person? Or gotten alcohol poisoning and died. Either way I would've been better off.

I sit in the cafeteria that smells really horrible, doing some sort of group with a dozen other people here. I'm not sure why the rest of these creature-people are in here but I don't want to ask. All the laces are missing from their shoes. I'm wearing black rubber flip-flops. I don't remember putting them on. The last shoes I remember wearing were heels. As least I don't look as retarded as the others.

My assignment is to draw a picture of what we think about our future life. Crayons, markers and construction paper are spread out on the table. I grab a piece of paper and a few markers. I don't do crayons. They make me feel like a child and get my hands greasy. I'm careful of what I draw. I want it to be dripping of happiness and positivity, so it will get back to that mean doctor that I have been behaving, and then I'll get released early.

On the paper I draw a picture of the world. Then add some hearts and a peace sign. The man nurse asks us to share our drawings. I call him the man nurse because I still don't know what to call him.

"I drew the world because the world is at my fingertips and I drew a peace sign because I have and will continue to have inner peace. And the hearts represent being in love with my future boyfriend and the love of my friends and family." I sound really cliché but I can't think what else a positive person would say or draw.

Next, this scruffy guy in his forties shares. He wears the paper gown-clothes the hospital supplied that I won't be caught dead in. The gown was offered to me but I refused it and said I would just wear my clothes. The scruffy guy's drawing is done in crayon. It's a giant circle scribbled in with black and brown. A cliff or wall or something is below it. He says the back hole represents his life and the world. How it's "dark, bad and negative." The cliff is there because his future is "a dead end similar to death."

No wonder this idiot is locked in here. These people are all crazy and I don't belong here with them. What the hell is his problem? Does he want to say locked up in the loony bin? He'll probably get another three-day hold just for saying that, unless he checked *himself* in.

After group we're allowed to go to bed. Some people are staying up to socialize and stuff, but I want to sleep because once I fall asleep it will be tomorrow and closer to when I can leave. The man nurse asks if I want to take a Valium before bed. I want to scream "dear God no!" but instead politely decline.

The next morning my roommate wakes me up. She says I have to get up because I have to go to breakfast. I hurry and brush my teeth, then go to the cafeteria. I don't want to look bad and be late or look like I'm not cooperating.

The cafeteria still smells weird. I don't eat my breakfast because it doesn't seem sanitary. I drink a single-serving orange juice from a sealed carton. I eat an individual sealed package of peanut butter, using a pre-wrapped plastic spoon.

After breakfast we have a group meeting and then we do this check-in. They go around the room and ask us a few questions each. The man nurse is back again this morning. He must work here full time. He asks three other people if they felt safe last night and then turns to me.

"Did you feel safe last night?" he asks. I want to say no and that I was worried one of the crazy people were going to stab me in my sleep but instead—

"Yes, I felt very safe and still do," I say. This seems like the most normal thing to say. And seriously, this is a fucked-up question to ask in the first place. I will be meeting with that mean doctor tomorrow and the staff is going to be filling him in on how I've been doing, so if I seem really happy I might be able to leave after I meet with him. Twelve hours earlier than what is the usual policy.

There is some free time here. There are three very old books on the shelf. I take them all and read until I have to go to another group meeting or get my vitals checked or something else. All the books are terrible. I read the least terrible one. The plot doesn't make a lot of sense but it still helps me. It distracts my mind from my own thoughts, so I don't have to feel or most importantly, think. When I read the words on the page I'm transported into a world which is nothing like my own. I can think about the life of the characters and their worries and problems. The other people watch the news, talk and do crossword puzzles, but I hate the news; it makes me cry.

It's the next day and I've just finished meeting with that mean doctor. The man nurse comes over to me while I'm reading. He says I can leave at 5 p.m. It's 10:30 a.m. and I won't have to spend another night here. I tell him I'm going to call my mom.

"I am allowed to leave at three so get here a little before that," I tell her on the phone.

Then he tells me if she can get here in time, I can leave after lunch at 1 p.m. He knows I've kept asking when I can leave and I'm not like the other people here who like this place for some reason. They've been here before, and seem to plan to be here again. I'm even happier now and tell him she will be able to pick me up at one.

I gather my stuff that the hospital has been keeping locked up somewhere. It isn't much. It's just the plastic bag of my jewelry and my purse.

Mother drives me to my apartment. "I got you out early but I had to make you an appointment with a therapist to get you officially released," Mom shoves a piece of paper at me with the time and the therapist's name. "You have to go and you better not flake out." She's mad at me. "I don't know what to do with you anymore. You're going to therapy for at least a month. I don't even know what to say. I don't understand this," she says.

I'm not sure what to say to her. I figured she would be mad. I don't really want to look at her either. I'm scared of her.

She says, "I don't have the energy for this. I had to drive really far to get here and I don't know why they brought you to this hospital. It's ridiculous. Then I was trying to pay and they wanted my insurance card and I couldn't find it. Had to spend an hour looking for it and now my office is a mess. I got a referral for you to go to this lady and I want you to go. This doesn't include the address, you're going to have to look it up."

"I'm sorry," I say. At this point I don't know what else there is to say. I also nod that I hear her and will do what she says. That's usually the best way to deal with her and her goddamn mood swings. Nothing she says is fucking new, but it doesn't mean I still don't wish she could show some motherly compassion or whatever. I did just get out of an embarrassing, traumatizing situation that I won't forget for the rest of my life.

"And I think I have an eating disorder," I say and think, along with whatever else is wrong with me.

"I know you do. Did you think I didn't know? Did you think Ashley didn't know?" she says.

She waits for my answer but I just sit there, holding my purse in my lap.

"This therapist I arranged for specializes in eating disorders. I'll email you her website," she finishes.

And that was that. She could have at least told me she knew I had an eating disorder because I didn't know until now.

"Maybe if you'd eaten that day you drank so much none of this would have happened to begin with," she says.

"Fine, I'll look at the woman's website tonight and call

to confirm my appointment," I say just to end the conversation. I've had a tough enough weekend, or life, to begin with.

# 12. UNFORGIVEN

I go to the therapist's office and am late, although it doesn't really matter. She obviously won't be able to help. I'm definitely beyond that. Besides, I've been to a therapist and psychiatrist before and it didn't work. But I do make sure to go because I don't want to be sent back to the loony bin, so I better adhere to whatever rules they have.

I was going to shower and get ready but now don't have time. I arrive in my worn-out workout clothes, five minutes late. I fill out the paperwork as fast as I can.

The therapist's name is Maggie. I like her energy but she is very thin, so in comparison I feel huge. I explain why I'm here. About my little accident, how I binge drank and wanted to hurt myself. Also that I couldn't exercise in the mental institution, so I did extra today to make up for it and that is why I am late. I did feel strange and slightly out of it at the gym today, like maybe some alcohol was still in my system. But I had to get my workout done.

I tell her I've been to a psychiatrist before so I'm used to this. Tell her more about my binge drinking and ask her what kind of therapy she does because I only believe in certain kinds. Like I believe in changing your thoughts 'cause that's what I used to do. She's a licensed marriage and family therapist. That's good 'cause I'm done with taking medication and in the past I never believed it really worked. I tell her I had to come to get out of the hospital. That "I'm not sure this is going to be a good fit." I might just come for this one appointment because I don't really want to do therapy.

"Do you think I have an eating disorder?" I say.

"Tell me your recent thoughts about food."

"I've been stressed because I want to be an actress but am a very nervous person and this showcase we were doing at school made me panic." Sitting here I think of that time a month ago that I tried to make myself throw up. Should I tell her? The image of me in my bathroom comes into my mind.

I tell her I worry I overeat. I don't want to eat tomorrow and yes, I know it's wrong but I still want to do it. That I just want to drink a lot of coffee, "this certain brand I drank today that made me sick and took away my appetite," I say and explain more about my eating.

She tells me I definitely do have an eating disorder. She further explains that an eating disorder is very, very serious. That it becomes extremely ingrained in people and takes a lot of therapy to treat, that most people need a three-pronged approach, including a dietitian and a psychiatrist.

"I don't know if I should keep coming. I don't think this or really anything will work 'cause I've already tried everything."

"I think you should, and an eating disorder never just fades away," Maggie says.

"But maybe I don't have one for sure because sometimes or for a while I don't do the things I was explaining."

She says that that's how eating disorders are. They can come in waves and go into hibernation, but they always come back and never go away by themselves. That the only way to recover from an eating disorder is dealing with the feelings. That an eating disorder is a *destructive* coping mechanism for pent-up feelings. It starts out helping and then after a while it doesn't work anymore and even makes things worse. I need to learn *constructive* coping mechanisms.

"I want to stop bingeing and be in control with food," I say.

She says I can and, "It's possible." I find her awfully hard to believe at this point. We make another appointment. I go home and binge and then run for two hours. The whole time my stomach is cramping and I feel dizzy. Our conversation has overwhelmed me.

I wake up on my couch. I look at the time. I am going to be late for my second appointment with Maggie. She gave me a bunch of homework assignments but I really didn't have time to do them because I was busy exercising, and was tired from being so overwhelmed and for other reasons I don't know.

I arrive late. Maggie says I missed half my session. But I was asleep; what was I supposed to do? We agreed I'd see her once a week for a long session because that was all I could afford, even though she wanted me to come more. I tell her I didn't do my homework either. So she's mad at me and I'm mad at her back. Doing it won't work anyway to help me, so I didn't see the point.

"I want to know what to do to stop bingeing," I say.

She tells me since I didn't do my homework it's hard for her to give me coping skills. That her treatment plan comes from how I feel and who I am specifically. Part of it was to journal about how I feel in my daily life. We spend the rest of the session discussing why I didn't do my homework. I leave feeling like a completely horrible person.

I run errands and then start my work right away for the next week. I begin to journal about myself and about food. Make a list of changes I want in my life, as well as do my life chart. Maggie explained to me how to do it. So I tape several pieces of paper together and then draw a long line across the page and write out my age every few inches, one to 21. I am supposed to write the most significant things, events and memories in my life on my chart, at the age they happened. Everything, the worst things to the best things.

I see Maggie for the third time and share my journaling with her along with the rest of my homework. She tells me to meet with a dietitian.

"I mean I guess I don't want to go. I've had a nutritionist before and they'll tell me what to eat, give me a diet plan or whatever. I know I won't be able to follow it," I say. But still, I tell her I'll call the dietitian.

Maggie is now able to give me some new skills. She teaches me deep breathing and we practice it in the session. I tell her I'm not sure I believe in this kind of thing, but we agree to do it and agree I'm willing to try it.

I do deep breathing in the car while driving and at stop lights. Yes I do. I'm determined to relax and not be anxious. I take deep breaths before I eat and can even pause while I'm eating and do breathing.

If I have to admit it, I do miss Penn, more than I've ever missed anyone in my life. It's just that I've come to the conclusion I'm too sick now to even be able to think about working with him or to imagine him seeing me as a woman. I doubt he would think I'm beautiful and sexy. If not sick physically, than mentally I am. I've dropped to a different level. I still want to be an actress but besides that I'm completely lost. I feel so gross and especially ugly. I don't remember feeling this ugly before I was in recovery. The thought of cuddling with any guy or kissing one makes me angry. Let alone one seeing and kissing my naked body. My body's sensations tell me I'm physically ready for this but my mind is not. It's not fair that they don't match and it doesn't make any sense. My sex drive is so strong. I feel it all over and nothing kills it but the rest of me disagrees. I wish to not have these feelings at all and that they'll go away. They just make everything more complicated.

I can't help but fantasize about him. I image us in a warm room where it's as light as a dark restaurant, we're making out, it feels so pleasurable, we both heat up, he's taking my clothes off…but these pleasures happen in other people's lives, not mine. I play along with this kind of life when people talk about their wives and boyfriends but beneath my pretending, this topic's humiliating to face. When I cry over him which is often now—at first I never cried—it's because I miss talking to him and more. Penn doesn't know about the eating disorder.

While shopping I see a T-Shirt with a Triumph motorcycle on it. The kind he had and want to buy it and wear it. I get mad at myself wondering why I didn't spend more time with him while he was here. I look up on the internet to see how much a plane ticket will cost to visit him in Zürich. I can't help myself. The tickets are astronomical and we don't have the kind of relationship where we will travel just to see each other. This makes me cry as well. I'm in a horrible mental space. A part of me doesn't want him to see me anyway. I don't want him to think I'm crazy.

His email says: *I got back from visiting my dad a couple weeks ago. Check out these pictures,* attached are a bunch of pictures taken near his dad's, landscapes of nature. But I thought he wasn't close with his dad. *When are you coming back to visit?* I write back to him. He responds vague, that he doesn't know yet.

I see Maggie for the fourth time.
"Why haven't you called the dietitian?" she says.

I don't really know what to say. It's not because I'm lazy or anything like that. It's because I know it won't work. So I didn't call, so I won't have to be let down twice as much when I do it, and it still doesn't work. We talk about this for a while and I end up committing to call.

I call the dietitian and make an appointment. Her office is near my apartment.

Walking to my dietitian's appointment I worry about being late. I jumped rope for forty-five minutes yesterday. Now my calves are so sore and tight that it hurts to walk, it hurts with every step. I can't walk normally. Actually I can barely walk at all. I parked on the street at a meter and now have to walk all the way to the building, inside and down the hall. The pain shoots up to the tendons above my knee. The pressure of every step rises to my calves, knees and shins. I haven't jumped rope since grade school but people say it burns a lot of calories, so I decided to do it.

Courtney gives me a list of groceries to buy. One week of meal and snack ideas, tells me to eat things like a peanut butter and jelly sandwich with a hand full of grapes. She doesn't even tell me what kind of bread to buy, if it should be whole grain, or what the amount of fiber should be.

"Do you have mayonnaise and mustard, hummus or peanut butter?" Courtney asks.

"I can't buy peanut butter because I'll eat the whole jar at once and I don't have the other things. Plus, I was on this diet where the only other thing you could eat, pretty much besides fruit and vegetables, was peanut butter, so I ate it all the time. And that diet just made me gain a ton of weight and I was always hungry and my stomach always hurt."

We add condiments to my list.

All that's in my fridge is skim milk and egg whites in a box so I go to the store to buy everything Courtney told me to get. Maybe it would be nice to eat an apple. An apple

118

with cheese is one of the snack ideas. Because I've stopped eating fruit altogether and have been just sticking to protein foods. I've been eating more protein so it will keep me full. Because of my high protein intake, the times I overeat won't change my body composition. See, it takes the body more energy to digest protein than other foods so it makes me burn more calories. In the end this keeps my body fat percentage low.

The grocery list didn't seem very long to begin with, but I am almost done shopping and the cart is full of food. I am scared about buying so much because I think I'll eat it all at once. I haven't bought this amount and this variety of food since I can remember. When I get the tortillas I'm not sure which kind I am allowed to buy because Courtney didn't say. I read the labels. One has hydrogenated oil and the other has high-fructose corn syrup. I don't know what kind to get. Maybe I should call Courtney and ask her, but I am afraid so I just buy the ones that are medium sized and cheap even though I don't feel comfortable getting them. I have so many things to get on my list. I don't have time to track every ingredient or brand.

I go home and make a meal on the list. It's a turkey wrap with a side of strawberries. That's why I need the tortillas. The wrap is made with a tortilla and inside is turkey, hummus, lettuce, tomato and cheese. Normally I won't eat this, won't eat the tortilla because I don't eat straight carbs unless they're in a protein bar. Won't eat hummus because there's oil in it and I save the fat in my diet for the impending binge I know will happen. I won't eat lettuce or tomato because I don't find these vegetables that tasty. So I leave them out of my diet to save the calories for things I really love, because I don't have that many calories I'm allowed to eat to begin with. Won't eat cheese because it's a high-calorie food with too much fat again, and dairy causes a rise of hormones in my body that makes my skin break out. Won't eat turkey because of the additives in it that wreak havoc on my body and I never trust that the organic kind is really a hundred percent organic so there is no safe turkey to eat.

After I eat the wrap with a side of strawberries I am full. I don't want to eat a second or third or fourth wrap, which is normally the case. It was really good. It tasted better than the one food I've been eating lately, eggs whites with black pepper and no salt.

I tell Maggie what Courtney taught me about food, and that my eating was better this week because of the meal plan she gave me.

I go see Courtney again. I have not jumped rope since that awful jump roping incident, but my calves are still in pain and feel very tight, so they haven't recovered yet. I am supposed to bring a specific brand of candy bar to the session, the kind I've been overeating on lately. I want to buy it right before the appointment, because I am afraid that if I buy it earlier, I will just end up eating it. So my plan is to get it right before, but I always have trouble timing things like this because I worry I'll be late. I get to the appointment late.

We talk about not going too long without eating and that I should keep snacks in my car. I tell her how my eating went this week. I take out my notebook that she gave me, where I am supposed to write down what I eat. But I only wrote about half the things I ate. I mean I guess I didn't really have time and it's a pain in the ass to do anyway. I really didn't see the point because I've been writing down what I eat and the calories for the past year and it never even helped me. But I tell her that the meal plan did help after all. Courtney asks me to take out the candy bar that I was supposed to bring and I do. It is a Hershey's white chocolate bar.

"Are you hungry?" she asks. I think very hard about this for a while.

"I don't know." I really don't know and don't understand why she asked me the question to begin with anyway. "I think a little," I say.

"Do you want to eat the chocolate?"

"I don't really know, not really. But if I was alone I probably would want it and would eat it." Courtney leaves the room to test me. She goes outside the office, waits five minutes and then comes back in.

"I didn't get the urge to eat it, even when you left."

"I want you to look at the package without opening it and tell me what you remember it tasting like and what you remember the texture feeling like in your mouth," Courtney says.

"I remember it tasting really good and really sweet. The texture was thick but soft and a little creamy I guess."

"Does the taste remind you of anything in your life? Are there any memories attached to it?"

I think of Penn because sometimes I'll imagine kissing him, and in my imagination he always tastes like Hershey's white chocolate. I also thought of a time when my mom yelled and screamed at me like a maniac, for absolutely no reason, while I was moving once. After she left, I went to the store, bought two bags of Hershey's white chocolate Hugs, and ate them all.

"Do you want to eat it now?" Courtney asks.

I look at the chocolate bar in my hand. "No, I don't want to. In fact, it's kind of grossing me out."

A week goes by and nothing really happens but for some unknown reason my eating is horrible again, and I binge a lot. One binge is really bad. It happens the way it always does. It is the end of the day. I've gone to the gym in the morning and eaten good all day. I've done a bunch of things on my to-do list, and am even having a productive day. Then this feeling comes over me and I am suddenly starving as if I have literally not eaten in months. It comes on in a millisecond. First I ignore it. The ignoring doesn't work. I fantasize about what I want to eat: Reese's peanut butter cups. I decide to go buy them. I tell myself it's okay because for the next few days I will exercise twice as much to make up for it and this will be the absolute last time I'll do it. Then I get hungrier and want to buy even more. Then tell myself I don't care. Fuck it and fuck everything. I am going to eat as much and whatever I want right now. That is the end of the millisecond. And the binge has already got me.

I go to the grocery store and buy three bags of Reese's cups, go home and eat all seventy-two. I want to slow down and eat but can't. I want to eat neatly but can't. I eat all the candy in under ten minutes. The only reason I know how many I've eaten is 'cause I count the wrappers after. Then calculate the calories I ate, seven thousand, five hundred and sixty three, to figure out how much I will have to starve myself for the next week to not gain weight.

After, the same feeling rushes over me like it always does, guilt and shame as if I've murdered someone. It may sound extreme or odd but that is the closest comparison there is. There is the desperation that I don't know what is wrong with me, and the disgust and humiliation of what I am. Then I just hate myself. I lie in bed for two and a half hours in too much pain to move. I get out of bed, and to put the final nail in the coffin, I measure my body fat on my body fat scale. It has risen by three point four percent.

I tell Maggie all this.

"I woke up this morning and I was so swollen that my eyes were almost swollen shut. I tried to drink a lot of water to counteract the swelling but it didn't work. I didn't even want to come today because I feel so ugly and like it's going to be impossible for me to get better. I still feel really bloated, and really fat and last night the bloating was so bad that it went up to my chest and I felt like I couldn't breathe," I say.

Usually I don't know what to say when I get to therapy

and it's awkward and I don't understand why she doesn't lead things. But today I know what to say right away.

"Why didn't you call me?" Maggie asks and I don't know what to say. She reassures me that my body is just holding water from the amount of food I've eaten and the swelling will go down.

"I bought granola bars to eat in the car so I wouldn't go too long without eating, get really hungry and then binge, but ended up bingeing in the car at stop lights on them."

"I think you need more support," Maggie says. She repeats what she had said to me in our first session that I need to go to a residential treatment program. "I was worried you didn't have enough support, it takes a lot of support to fight an eating disorder."

I really don't understand what she means by using this "support" word all the time.

"Now I think you're right," I say, meaning that now I know I need to go to the hospital or whatever it's called. The first time Maggie brought this up I told her she was overreacting and "I'm not that bad" and it was too expensive anyway. I'd even called my insurance to check the price.

"I'm done living like this and I want to go to a live-in treatment center," I say. Maggie has three recommendations of where I should go. I get out my notebook and write them down as well as what city they're in.

"Research these places and we'll talk about what to do next week or we can make an appointment for you to come in sooner," Maggie says. She tells me she will help me every step of the way. That she has walked other people through this and it's gone well.

I get on the internet and look at the treatment facilities. One place keeps talking about spirituality and getting in touch with it, and how it helps your recovery. It has a pretty website. The second place is in Oregon and is the most expensive of all three. The last one talks mostly about the structure of the program. All three of them have Frequently Asked Questions pages, so I go to them, but all the questions seem to be dealing with not being able to eat instead of not being able to *stop* eating. What the food is like. What they do if you are a vegetarian and how much weight you should gain each week. Again, I don't really get why these are Frequently Asked Questions and what they have to do with me. Do I not need to go away to treatment after all? Because the types of eating disorders the websites talk about don't seem like what I have.

I bring back my research to Maggie.

"I want you to plan to stay for six weeks to three months," Maggie says.

I'm shocked by this and thought it would only be 30 days like I've seen in the movies or heard about from people who went to rehab for drugs. Plus, most of the websites say 30 days. She also tells me the longer I stay the better, and that it usually takes the first month just to adjust.

I tell Maggie I want to go to the place called Sea Breeze. It is the one that talks about the structure and schedule of the program. I don't really tell her why I choose it, but I know why, because the place in Organ is too expensive and I cross the other place off my list because it talks about spirituality. So Sea Breeze is left. Talking with Maggie, it comes up that I probably won't be allowed to exercise there. And I start to freak out. She notices my face.

"Is something wrong?" Maggie says.

I want to tell her absolutely everything about this entire situation is wrong, but I don't.

"I didn't know I wouldn't be allowed to exercise," I say.

"I'm not a hundred percent sure, but that most likely will be the case."

"I'm worried about my running time increasing and that I'll gain a ton of weight and get fat," I say.

Maggie tells me she thinks I over-exercise. I don't know

why because I haven't even talked about exercise that much, except for my journaling I read to her. Is it because I usually come to my appointment still in my workout clothes?

"How much time do you spend exercising in a week?" Maggie asks.

"About an hour and a half, six days a week and I've cut down a lot recently, because it was twice that much a few weeks ago." But she says I still exercise too much. I mention my running time again.

"Lots of people change while they're away. Their priorities change too and you might not care about your running time when you get back," she says.

At home, I call Sea Breeze. They say if exercise is something helpful to me it will be allowed and incorporated into my schedule. I decide I'll go, but know deep down this is probably a mistake.

The next time I see Maggie I ask what I should pack. She tells me lots of people wear sweats while they're there. This makes me feel depressed. I imagine going to this very dull place with grey walls. Everyone running around in their pajamas and never even getting ready for the day and being all frumpy. I don't even own sweat pants. Just workout pants that I wear to the gym.

# 13. FIGHT CLUB

## Week 1

Today I'm checking into the residential treatment program, Sea Breeze, for my eating disorder. It's not a building or medical office like I imagined. It looks just like a normal house because it is. It's just a regular house, in a regular neighborhood.

I park in the driveway. My mother is waiting outside the house. I'm three and a half hours late. I hurry and start walking to the front door. Mom stops me before I get there. She seems to want to talk to me about something.

"What? We have to go in now. I'm already late," I say.

"I don't want you to ever say 'Mom sounded drunk.'"

Now I know what she is talking about, probably something I told my cousin. See, I called my mom to talk about the insurance while we were arranging for me to check into Sea Breeze. On the phone, she was practically incoherent and sounded completely out of it. I mean, I was pissed because this was a serious situation to begin with and I was running around arranging everything. Mom said she wanted to help because I got the wrong information from the insurance company, and then she goes and fucks it all up when I needed to talk to her.

I continue to rush to the house, walking past her 'cause I'm so late and she won't let this go. I can't believe she's talking about this now, especially while I'm so tardy.

"I could hardly understand you on the phone."

"I'm talking about the way you treat me," she says.

"Fine. I won't do it again," I say, to get her off my back.

She's bringing this up *now*! Doesn't she get what's going on and that this is a completely inappropriate time? The front of the house has a pond and looks just like the picture on the website. I finally walk in. The house is open with tall ceilings. Inside, I'm led through the entryway to the living room. My mom, who has already been inside, follows behind me. I sit on the white couch where a woman named Jessica tells me to have a seat. There are papers and forms spread out on the coffee table.

"Do you have a cell phone?" Jessica asks.

"Yes," I say.

"Okay, you can give it to us."

I look at my mother.

"You're supposed to relax here and not be bothered," Mom says, encouraging me to give up my phone.

I fish my phone out of my purse and hand it to Jessica. I sign what seems like two thousand forms. I'm very tired and haven't slept all night. I repress a yawn. Some forms say I won't harm myself and other forms say that I voluntarily commit to the rules of the program. After I sign the papers, I say goodbye to my mother. Give her an awkward hug and she leaves. Jessica introduces me to the dietitian.

The dietitian leads me into another room in the house and starts grilling me with questions. I worry I may fall asleep in the loveseat that I'm sitting on. She sits on the bed across from me. When is this going to be over so I can go to bed? My eyes burn, and are glazing over but I don't know what to tell her. I don't want the people here to think I'm disobedient and uncooperative. She asks me if I have any forbidden foods.

"I'm not sure what you're talking about," I say.

"Foods that you don't let yourself eat or foods that you fear because you want to eat them, but you don't think are 'safe.' Or maybe you worry you'll overeat on them. If you eat them at all?" she asks.

I think about this. There aren't really any foods I don't let myself eat. Recently I let myself eat all kinds of food. I thought this would help me feel satisfied with food and help me lose weight, but it didn't.

"I guess I eat too many Reese's Pieces. Lots of times I don't want to eat them, but I end up eating them," I say.

"Are you hungry now? The other girls are going to be having night snack in a few minutes. Do you want to join them?" She asks.

"Yes." On top of not sleeping, I haven't eaten either because I was too anxious to eat all day, even though I meant to follow my meal plan. I made a meal on it but could only get myself to eat a few bites because I was feeling so sick. Now I feel like shit.

"What do you want to eat?" she asks.

"I guess a peanut butter and jelly sandwich. I don't know how to eat anymore. I just said 'peanut butter and jelly' because that's a food my old dietitian had me eat."

I eat my peanut butter and jelly sandwich. I eat fast as I'm starving. The staff and other clients or patients, whatever I'm supposed to call them, grill me with questions as well. I give as many one-word answers as possible because this uses the least amount of energy.

It's 10:30 p.m. and I'm in what will be my room, I guess. I don't know why I can't go to bed. I do ask, but Jessica says she has to count my stuff first. I can't think well enough to argue this point, or say I didn't sleep the whole night. As I'm running on fumes and not quite sure what's going on, I switch to survival mode. Wait until this is over. Sit on the bed.

Jessica opens my suitcase and starts counting things. She counts my shirts, pants, underwear, *everything*. She looks at my makeup. Takes seventy-five percent of it because it "has alcohol in it," including my favorite toner. She takes my razor, tweezers, plus all my workout equipment I need. I had packed a medicine ball, two jump ropes, resistance bands, a yoga mat and a heart rate monitor. Also a tape measure and two different types of body fat calipers. She leaves the room to get another container for my confiscated stuff, since it wouldn't all fit in the one she brought. The intake guy dropped the ball on the list of stuff I wasn't allowed to bring. He told me he would email it to me, but then said it wasn't that important and there weren't that many restrictions.

Jessica talks about the brands of my clothes. Like this is no big deal and we're girlfriends. I don't know what to think about this. Don't know how to act in rehab. I'm finally allowed to go to bed. I fall asleep instantly.

I'm awakened by someone. They tell me to take a shower. I'm a little out of it so I do as they say. In the shower, I realize I didn't bring my shampoo so I use whatever is there. I hope it's okay. I brought my clothes into the bathroom. As I'm putting on my shirt they knock on the door, yell something through it. They say it's time for breakfast. It's 7:30am. I feel rushed and that I have no privacy.

I eat eggs and toast. Regular eggs, not egg whites and the toast has real butter on it. I'm told something about not being allowed in the kitchen. After breakfast they take my blood pressure and something else. Then they give me my food and feeling chart and tell me to fill it out. I write that during breakfast I felt tired and anxious.

I wait until 4 p.m. today when I am allowed to use the phone to call Maggie. I look around before I get on the phone. The staff is in the other room. They are preparing for dinner. We eat three meals and three snacks a day. There is a big living room around the phone area. So I don't worry someone can hear me. I tell Maggie I don't like it here and that this place sucks. That I should leave and go somewhere else because the staff are stupid and unqualified.

"I think you should stay and if you leave you might not get approved by your insurance to go somewhere else. It could still really help. The worst that can happen is you won't binge for a month or two."

I guess she has a point.

I tell Maggie more about how it's going. That I'm too drained to learn anything and have been falling asleep in group therapy.

"I'm glad you went and it's okay if sometimes you don't hear everything that's talked about because you're so tired. You'll get some of it." Maggie says.

Maggie says she's glad I called, and I'm happy I got to talk to her. I really like her but don't know if she's right. I decide I'll stay here until the end of the week, but most likely leave then.

## Week 2

I wake up before everybody else to beat them to the shower. It has run cold on me the last week. I shower as fast as I can now. It goes cold still. I finish in the cold, pissed.

Today, I don't plan my meals ahead of time. I do it right before each meal and have only thirty minutes to do it. I hate it because I'm always rushed. I told the treatment team I wasn't ready for this but they disagreed and made me do it anyway. At lunch I couldn't decide what to eat and ended up eating two slices of cheese, a half cup of rice, carrots, a granola bar, milk and olives to make sure I got in all the units I needed for the meal: starches, fruit, protein, dairy and fat. But the "meal" didn't really resemble a meal at all. It was an odd snack at best. I was supposed to be learning to eat normally and not disordered.

I'm not allowed in the kitchen yet because I've only been here a week. The others are because they've been here longer, so they have more clearance. Food is served to me. We eat dinner. I eat off of a placemat an old patient made and left behind. All the other girls have their plate on a placemat that they collaged and laminated. I haven't made a placemat like I am supposed to. As I think this assignment is lame and I'm not doing it.

All the anorexics get to eat more than I do. I detest them because later I'll have to hear them complain about how much they have to eat. I eat all my food even though I don't have to. I only have to eat 75 percent. The anorexics have to eat a 100 percent.

"You didn't finish your hummus," the current babysitter on duty says to one of the anorexics. I call the staff members babysitters sometimes because that's what it feels like they are.

"I ran out of crackers so I have nothing to puts the hummus on. You want me to just eat a spoonful of hummus?" the anorexic says.

"You can eat plain hummus. There's just a little left."

We aren't allowed to talk about food at the table while we eat but sometimes the rules are broken. The anorexic complains some more. She finally finishes her hummus.

After dinner we have "free/journal time" before it's time for night snack. I sit in the "TV/craft room" with a girl named Debra. She arrived only a few days before me.

We get to talking. She says she ate too much at dinner and feels really full. I wonder how. I ate everything and am still hungry. She is on "75 percent." So she doesn't have to eat everything. She only ate a little over the minimum she was required. She tells me she used to be anorexic and says it was easier then, and it's embarrassing and humiliating to say she binges. That she'd rather say "compulsively overeat." I practically jump up off the couch because I agree with her exactly, and tell her my eating disorder is humiliating to talk about and have.

This morning before breakfast I ask for a cup of water from the kitchen. They bring it to me. I drink the whole cup pretty fast. Well, apparently pretty fast because one of the guards tells me to not do that again because it can be a way of repressing my appetite before I eat. I wasn't doing what he thought I was. Just really thirsty and shouldn't have gotten in trouble.

Later I ask if I can exercise and am told no by my babysitter. I don't understand because the intake guy said I'd be allowed to work out if I thought it helped me cope. A deep sense of betrayal hits me. He would have told me anything to get me to check into this place. I know this residential house, although it takes insurance, is a commercial establishment. He better not work on commission. I don't know how that would be legal.

I read the Sea Breeze exercise rules written in black and white that everyone has and learn the truth that I can't exercise. He wanted my money and was completely lying and manipulating me to get it. He knew the rules to this place and there is no middle ground. My insurance didn't even cover me to come here. They denied me, and by "denied" I really mean "fucked." They said I wasn't sick enough. So my mother will be getting the bill, $1,800 a day.

We go to the park. I'm thinking if I can't exercise then I will walk around for 12 minutes to get a little exercise in. I plan where I'll walk in the park. Find a long section of grass. That's the area that I can go to. A staff member sees me walking and comes over to me.

"You need to sit down," he says referring to a bench. I sit. I'm so angry and hate him for controlling every move I make. But I do as I'm told and sit down on it. I don't like parks. They're dirty. I'm in trouble again. I wait here, almost about to fall asleep until it's time to leave.

Every day I'm tired. My favorite part of the day is after night snack at 8:30 p.m. because then I'm allowed to go to sleep. I always go to bed right after snack because I'm so exhausted, but seem to be the only one who does this. In bed, I put in my earplugs so I don't have to hear anyone. The door isn't allowed to be shut. So it's left open but I turn off the light. Yes, this is my favorite time of day.

## Week 3

I wake up first again in attempts to get any warm water. I go to Shawn, our main babysitter, to check out my razor, toner and tweezers. I remind him to let my razor dry before it's locked up after I shower, to save the moisture stick. I pack up some old paperwork after breakfast because it's Tuesday. We take medical labs every Tuesday after breakfast to check our vitamin levels, hormones and all that. I want to have something to do in the waiting room.

Wednesday I sit at breakfast and watch one of the anorexics eat. I've already finished my food so I watch her. Anorexic Rachael eats cereal. My jaw tightens seeing how she eats it because she puts so little on her spoon. How will she ever finish the bowl by the time meal is over? And she will get in trouble if she doesn't eat it by then. So I watch her, and play this game with myself that she won't be able to because practically no food is coming out of the bowl. The staff add to my jaw pain as well as make a pain shoot up my back. They should tell her to put normal portions on her spoon and that she's not eating normally. Breakfast is over. Rachael finished the bowl, God knows how. I'm tired now from being mad for so long.

The next day at the table my food tastes delicious. I can't remember the last time I went so long eating normally, even though I tried all the time. Can't believe I'm allowed to eat all these different kinds of food. I eat yogurt, mix fruit in it, add dried apricots and one tablespoon of cashews, plus one serving of bacon, which is three slices.

I can't stand the table games they have us play. They're ludicrous and always about naming a "celebrity" or actor. They always upset me because they remind me that I don't have an acting career yet, because of the fact that I'm scared and nervous and don't really go on any auditions, and because I'm worried I'll fail. Acting is everything to me. So it's not like a normal failure. It's like this desperate ache-in-my-body failure that I'll never get over and that nothing can come close to replacing. So at the table, I make sure to talk a lot and make conversation to keep away the "celebrity" talk. I ask what we're going to do later today. I complain that the house is always cold and I'm freezing. I'm excited to watch a rerun of *The Sopranos* that's on tonight, right between dinner and night snack. But I can only hold the conversation for so long and then they go back to table games. I never participate.

## Week 4

I'm actually awake today, maybe the first day I've been awake since I got here. I don't zone out in any of the groups or fall asleep. I don't even feel the need to close my eyes when I am sitting on the couch.

Lisa, my roommate is awesome. She's very artistic like me and has all these hobbies and interests and just graduated from college. She dresses so cute and original, and is doing great eating all her meals and restoring her weight.

Katie, the weird client, is still weird, but Lisa has warmed to her because she's nicer than me.

Debra's the baby of the group because she's only eighteen. Debra and I talk all the time now. She's so sweet and jokes that every night she dreams she has a boyfriend. Lisa and I team up to build her confidence and don't let her beat herself up emotionally.

Rachel's eating habits don't make me want to scream as much anymore. She's been here the longest and is the wise one.

I learn the main types of an eating disorder in one of the group therapy meetings. Anorexia means they can't maintain healthy weight. They are underweight. Anorexics can also over-exercise, throw up and binge but their official term is "anorexic" and of course they restrict their food.

The other type is bulimic. It's where the person is at a healthy weight but "purges" by inducing vomiting or by over-exercising, and it's usually after a binge. The vicious cycle usually looks like this: restrict food by hardly eating and then overeat, which is the binge, and then get rid of the calories by purging. Anorexics and bulimics both obsess over food and how their body looks.

It's weird because before I knew I had an eating disorder, I thought an eating disorder was when someone just didn't eat at all or threw up what they ate. I didn't know that when the first thing on my mind was controlling and planning my food, that was a symptom. But now when I think about it, it's like being a junkie. The first thing on a junkie's mind is her next fix.

I think this is why it took me so long to realize I had an eating disorder, and I definitely didn't know there was such a thing as exercise addiction and that over-exercising is a "purge." That's never in magazines. I have bulimia! I sometimes compulsively overeat but I also restrict food and over-exercise. I pretty much self-destruct every way that's possible with food and exercise. And instead of throwing up, I'd over-exercise.

In another group meeting I learn more how my eating disorder helped me "cope" with how bad I felt. When I would starve myself by "restricting," that was so I wouldn't have to feel anything. I could be numb. When I would "binge" that was so I could soothe the pain I was feeling. When I would over-exercise I would "purge," which was when I was getting the icky feeling out of me.

A new girl arrives. Her name is Geneva. She's a mom.

I'm in the living room journaling when she says goodbye to her daughter. The little girl looks about five. Geneva's crying. I don't want to watch. I want to be back at Strasberg. Back at my normal life, back rehearsing and on stage. I wish Rourke was giving me a hard time on a scene I did and telling me I should've known better.

The little girl isn't sad like her mom. She says goodbye with a smile on her face and is holding a stuffed blue monkey. I still can't watch. I overhear the daughter's going to be left with her grandma. Where's her dad?

In group, Geneva talks about what brought her here and that her main self-destructive eating disorder behavior in the last two years has been restricting. Basically, she starves herself by constantly eating a very small amount of food. She tells us that she was fainting at work and was sent to the doctor, he said she would die in six months if she didn't start eating.

The groups are insufferable. They're completely devastating and I don't want to hear this stuff. I'm sensitive. I want to cry for her and at the same time don't know what's wrong with her. And I'm mad at her; how could she not check herself in sooner if she was fainting? I don't understand her. She doesn't even seem to want to be here. I'm not sure if she really cares that she could die in six months. These groups are horrible. I can't bear to watch her. She can't finish her meals, always has to supplement with nutrition drinks and complains she can't take all the food they're making her eat. It's fucking devastating. I hate it here again and want to leave immediately.

I worry how she'll ever recover, but you know what? Seeing her not able to eat makes it easier for me to eat and want to eat normally. I even ate a Reese's Pieces today and didn't even feel guilty. I even enjoyed it. I don't want to be her. I'd rather be dead. She's brainwashed that food is bad, and the only thing to live for is the external body. Why would she want to live like that? And how can her daughter not learn the same thing? How will she turn out whole? Maybe if Geneva doesn't recover, she'll lie to her daughter and pretend to be healed to protect her. I notice she kept her daughter's stuffed blue monkey. It lays on the couch in the milieu. I learn the "TV/craft room" is called the "milieu."

I pick up the monkey. I'm taken back to one night after rehearsing with Penn.

I think it was after dark at his apartment, near the end of the week, maybe a Thursday night. His window was open and it smelled like summertime. We'd fought earlier about shutting it or not. He'd won, so it was still open. I noticed his suitcase open and unzipped in the corner of his room. There were a couple of folded-up T-shirts inside.

"You started packing," I said.

"Why won't you let me hold you?"

"I thought guys didn't like to hold girls."

"That's true and that's not true. We want both. We want to hold a girl and look down at her in our arms and be next to her. And then we see a nice ass walking by and we want that too."

"Maybe this is why."

"Come lay next to me, just for a minute," he said.

"It won't be right for the scene."

"That's bullshit. Rehearsal's over."

Another memory flashed through my mind.

Penn had been trying to hold my hand across the table during rehearsal at Strasberg. I'd let him touch my hand and then move it away. He'd wait a minute and then take it back. Penn accidently made a joke out of one of his lines; he'd been trying to seriously motivate it and make it authentic, but it came out really funny. I started cracking up and then so did he. We couldn't stop laughing for ten minutes.

I drop the stuffed monkey back on the couch.

Two of the damn anorexics are complaining that they aren't allowed to go on walks with us. I got approved. So now I'm allowed to walk for twenty minutes with the group when we go to the hiking trails. I'm still not permitted to have real exercise time but secretly a little part of me is glad that I can't because my body is worn out. Since *the staff* says I'm not allowed to exercise, I don't even have to feel guilty about it.

Anyway, the anorexics are practically freaking out that they have to sit down on the bench at the trails and journal. It's so annoying. I try to be sympathetic 'cause I can relate and understand a little, but they act like they almost don't want to get better. Don't they have common sense that they're so underweight they need to burn as few calories as possible to gain weight, and gain it faster? It's hard to even get to the feelings and what's underneath if they can't even do the first step. I wonder if they know how crazy they sound and look. Like they are being tortured to sit on a bench and look out at the ocean. It's weird, and you know what I actually don't understand it. They're not where I am. There are two kinds of people in recovery; the ones who want to get better and the ones who don't. And it's very clear who is who. I want to get better now, even if I will hate my body forever. At least I won't have to be hungry anymore. At least I won't be out of control. Hell, even if I weren't approved to walk, I'd sit on the goddamn bench with the anorexics and I wouldn't complain.

I write in my feeling and food chart before, during and after eating that I feel despair.

At one of the groups today, the female therapist leading talks about over-exercise and that it's a way to punish yourself. I'm shocked.

"Would you ever do that to someone else, starve them, make them exercise for hours or make them eat so much that they are in physical pain, and still make them do wind sprints?" she says.

I wonder what I was punishing myself for or why I would do that. I thought I like myself because I'm an artist and will never settle for a life I don't love, like most people.

Group is over. I take down vigorous notes to remember everything she said. I don't want to over-exercise anymore.

Then I remember the perfectionism group we had and stop taking notes because having so much emotional energy over forgetting one little thing is perfectionism in itself.

I never thought I was a perfectionist. I always thought that would be stupid to be because it's not realistic, even though Rourke always tended to believe I was. After learning about perfectionism, I think I've been acting out this compulsion with my life and my eating disorder. Perfectionism should be re-labeled from perfection to protection, because that's why I strive for it and why other people strive for it. It's the drastic search for what is wrong or just below extraordinary. It's tunnel vision, focused on what's broken. Apparently, I tried to be perfect so I would have a layer of armor on me, so nobody could break through and hurt me. When I was little, I was hurt so bad by being neglected and emotionally abandoned that I subconsciously put up walls since then. Like sometimes, I think about hard times in my life and how much I focused on the external during them. Now I know I did because I thought if I looked okay on the outside and was together on the outside, I could handle any crazy situation and any terrible feelings that were happening on the inside.

I'm taught all food is good in balance and moderation. I'm also taught about hunger and full signals. To eat when I'm hungry and stop eating when I'm full. It seems like a simple concept but it's not since I have an eating disorder. In fact, this notion could not be more foreign to me. I can hardly tell when I'm hungry or full because I never used to think about it and haven't done it in so long. Now I have to slow down and listen to the instincts in my body, and to not just stop eating because I've eaten the amount of calories I should eat. They don't let us count calories here. Sometimes they even black out the back of nutrition labels on salad dressings so we can't look at them. I have to realize when I am satiated and, only then, stop. It seems strange, but what they teach me here is *how* to eat or how to do it in a non-disordered way. It's hard.

## Week 5

I learn about a new feeling: loneliness. I thought my eating disorder was caused by my anxiety about auditioning. Now I think I feel lonely and don't know why. I don't like the feeling. It's stupid and weak and not a big deal. I don't see what it has to do with my career. So I don't know why I'm noticing it and giving it attention. On a good note, I've finally been approved for 20 minutes of exercise time, 5 days a week.

Katie, the odd girl that's here, arrived a few days after me. She keeps to herself as much as she's allowed and I haven't had a lot of interaction with her. I don't know much about her other than she's been in treatment before. She's had an eating disorder for a lot longer than I have. Katie always wears black. I mean always, black: shirt, pants, socks and shoes. I know she has black socks because she lifted up her pant leg one time to complain to the staff member how swollen she was from having to eat. Her legs looked childlike and seemed smaller than my arms. I didn't see any swelling. Also, I know this girl has a weird thing with showers. She has to take two a day. This is against the house rules. We're only allowed one. She takes one is the morning and one after lunch or dinner. They let her shower after a meal if the door is cracked open. A female staff member sits by it and reads so she can't purge in the toilet. Still, a part of me suspects she's throwing up in the shower drain. Why else would she always want another shower?

We sit at the table during dinner. I don't like my dinner. I eat it anyway because I am hungry. Anorexic Katie is next to me and eats her dinner which is beans, tofu, no sauce, no meat and no dairy. She's still using food rules. This is the way people with eating disorders take dieting to the extreme. Like if someone normal is on a diet, one of their diet rules may be "I'm trying to eat more vegetables every day." With eating disorders the way of eating is very radical, for example, "I only eat raw vegetables before 2 p.m." The number of rules in my own head was usually around 2,000 and they change frequently. Sometimes I would start a new diet once a week or have new food rituals every hour.

I'm sure Katie is using food rules because I've used all these ways to control food myself. So far I've counted three and I know if I tried I could think of more she's using. She picked all low glycemic foods, that's one. She's eating variety technically because she has different kinds of beans but really it's one food which equals the custom to only eat three different foods a day and only one or two at a time. There is no dairy in her meal, which is another rule, the false one that says dairy causes your body to store fat. She has plain tofu with no sauce. This bland food equals the food obsession where I have to know every ingredient I eat so I know it's safe. The many spices and ingredients in sauce make it unsafe. Overall, she picked a very controlled and disordered meal.

Dinner's technically over. We already put our plates in the kitchen. I say I don't want to watch a movie with the girls later because I want to use my exercise time. Katie says to me, "Because you have to exercise."

"Yeah, how would you feel if you didn't get your second shower of the day," I say back.

"How would you feel if you didn't get to exercise?" Katie asks again.

I walk into the kitchen and mumble under my breath that she's "a fucking bitch." Shawn, who's on duty, and Lisa, are there along with Katie. They give me a *stop that* look and I feel embarrassed and ashamed. I go to my room.

Maybe I do still have a problem with exercise and I don't want that. Later, I say "hey" to Katie as we walk past each other to use the bathroom before bed. She says "hey" back. I wanna be recovered. And Katie pointed out my problem to me.

The next afternoon I do an assignment for my dietitian to list all the food rules I used to use, and the ways I thought I would obsess over food. The ways I thought about it and how I would diet or try to eat less, my own personal ones.

I write down one rule, then more come to me. In the past, when I thought I was getting better, or thought I wasn't being weird with food anymore, I was just getting rid of one rule and picking up another. I guess the fancy term for this is denial.

### *Food Rules/Habits/Tendencies*

*~Take caffeine pills because they make me feel sick to my stomach and I will do anything that I think will repress my appetite – when I feel sick it makes me not want to eat*

~Drink a lot of coffee in hopes I'll have more energy to exercise

~Take an old prescription of Adderall that I was forced to take in high school to make me not want food

~Don't like to eat food unless it comes from a package

~At restaurants when the waiter asks for my menu after I order, I always ask to keep it so I can look at the pictures of the food and imagine eating everything I can't

~Don't like to leave any crumbs on the plate. Have to eat every last bit

~Have to eat every two hours exactly. I set a timer

~Can only eat a high-glycemic food if I eat it with a low glycemic food. Have to eat the low glycemic food first

~Chew my food until it's very mushy in my mouth, at least 25 chews

~Always buy the same brand of food. Have to know I like it and have eaten it before to be allowed buy it

~Have to know how many calories are in a food before I can eat it

~Only eat small snacks and small portions and never an entire meal at once

~Only eat carbs if they are with protein, and the grams of protein have to be equal or higher than the grams of carbs

~Have to eat all of the protein in a meal before the carbs

~Never drink my calories. Can't drink juice or anything like that

*~Have to like the utensils I eat with and use specific ones. Can't eat off paper plates because I worry the food will soak into the plate and I'll get less to eat*

*~Don't like to be around smells and/or candles that smell good because they make me want to eat*

*~Can't waste calories on anything I don't really love so if something doesn't taste just right in my mouth I spit it out*

*~Food has to be exactly 70 percent protein, 10 percent fat and 20 percent carbs*

*~Have to write down everything I eat and what time I eat it*

*~At night I can't fall asleep until three hours after I eat*

*~Have to know what every ingredient on a food package is. Have to have read about it and approved of it before I can eat it*

*~After 6 p.m., I can only eat protein foods*

*~My biggest meal of the day, and the meal with the most sugar and carbs has to be eaten in the morning when I first wake up*

I continue writing my list. Later, Lisa sees me and Katie come back from a walk. Katie had been approved to go on walks and wanted to get out. She wanders off and Lisa comes to talk to me.

"Did you guys make up?" she asks me.

"No, but we're good now," I say.

I'm in my individual therapy session. I always start the session and bring up what I want to talk about. I say I want to do all these things but am too tense to do them, so I avoid them and then hate myself for not doing them. But this time my therapist interrupts me halfway through my sentence.

"So tell me about what happened between you and Katie?" she asks.

"Oh, you heard about that," I say.

"Yeah the first thing I do when I come in is check up on everything I have missed and read the awareness log."

The awareness log is a journal or record the staff members keep on generally what happened each day with the clients.

"Oh, I see," I say.

I explain to her about what happened and that I got suddenly angry when Katie said that comment to me at the table. And then I got a little out of control with my response.

"Why do you think that is?" she asks.

"She called me out on my over-exercising."

This leads us into a conversation about my meal plan. My therapist says the treatment team will be raising my units because I have lost weight this week. The units are a general measurement on how many calories are healthy and normal for me to eat. They weigh us once a week, in the morning before breakfast and we have to put on these hospital gown things. They never tell us what we weigh and they have a special scale with an attached reader so we can't see the number.

"Your weight is borderline right now so if you lose any more weight you will actually be considered underweight," she says.

I understand what she is saying but have a hard time trusting her. She keeps mentioning what the charts say about weight range for my height, age, vitamin deficiency levels and other stuff like that. But the charts must be wrong. I want to ask to see the charts and the science behind all this but then think that could be the eating disorder part of my mind trying to take over. So I don't ask.

Maybe it will be okay that they're raising my units because I'm still hungrier than I think I should be. I don't want to malnourish myself because I know now that will just lead eventually to overeating.

## Week 6

I'm leaving at the end of the week and don't want to go. I don't want to leave all the girls. We have so much fun together. I'm safe from myself here and don't want to be back in the real world. I'm afraid the urge will come over me so strong to binge or over-exercise that I won't be able to fight it. I don't want to relapse. I'm not ready to go. I'm worried something will really upset me and I'll go straight to food. Scared my outpatient program won't be enough help and support. Nervous I won't be able to follow my meal plan, but Shawn and the other staff say it's good I'm concerned and am making a relapse prevention plan.

I have checked out of the program, ate my night snack and now it's time for me to drive home.

Driving home I look at my cell phone. It's been locked up most of the time. I've saved a text message from Penn, the one he wrote me when he sold his motorcycle. But instead of endings, beginnings come to my mind. My first day at Strasberg flashes through my brain. Crying, I left halfway through Rourke's class, but still showed up the next day and then kept showing up. My commitment to studying and rehearsing Method Acting only grew. Being angry at my mom and not knowing why flashes through my mind. The first time Rourke said I had talent. The first time I learned what body fat percentage was.

I plan what things I'll do tomorrow. The most important thing to do will be eating mindfully and following my meal plan. Tomorrow is Saturday and my outpatient program doesn't start until Monday.

# 14. MISERY

I make a sandwich. Am not really hungry but it is time to eat. I turn off the TV and sit at the kitchen table alone to eat mindfully and concentrate hard on feeling my hunger and full signals. It is one of my first meals on my own after leaving residential. I eat half of it but then start to cry on my grilled cheese because this is my existence. It's the first time I feel like an actual lowlife addict and realize this is my life now, living to not relapse. And this will be my life for god knows how long? Years? Sitting alone with no distractions and paying attention eating. But there is no room in my life right now besides recovery. I'll never go back to the way things were before.

At home in my apartment I go through my things, old papers and old clothes. Get rid of all my clothes that are too small and too big, which is basically my entire wardrobe. Donate all my diet books. Throw away papers and journals of my weight and body circumference measurements. Close my eyes as I throw them away to make sure I don't see any of the numbers. I get rid of my caffeine pills and the Xanax I stole from my roommate, Ashley, so I could sleep instead of eat, as well as the cans and tubs of protein powders and the caffeine-enhanced protein water left in the cupboard.

Penn and I still exchange emails occasionally and we've talked a couple of times on the phone. He asks for my mailing address in one email. I get a book in the mail. It's the first present I've ever gotten from a guy. It's about Method Acting.

"Rourke told us to get it when I was first in class with him. He used to recommend it," he tells me on the phone.

I like the sound of his voice. "He never mentioned it in my classes. I can't wait to read it."

"Why haven't you sent out your headshots?"

"I think mostly because I have this chronic fatigue. I'm trying things to fix it."

"That's a good excuse," Penn says.

"I'm not joking." *Since when is he my shrink?*

"Why don't you just send out two by next week and then call me after you have."

The next day I send out two headshots. Glad we made the agreement and that I have someone to talk to about this stuff. Still, I think I send them not for me but for him. So I have a reason to call. I should care about my headshots more. But again I'm in a strange place mentally and can't be tough on myself like I used to be. I have to baby myself so I don't fall apart.

"I sent them," I tell him on the phone.

"That's great! See it's not that bad." We talk some more but don't make another deal. It gets too late because of the time difference and he has to go.

For a meal I eat pizza and fruit salad. I eat the pizza until I'm full. It doesn't take that much pizza. Food tastes different now. I mean, I taste it but it's really not that good. I eat it and that's it and I'm glad I don't have to eat bland, gross food and be hungry all the time anymore. But I feel this dull grey cloud on everything. Even the gym is like that. I'm allowed to work out a little more now. I go to the gym, do a good workout and feel the same as I did before. Don't feel more beautiful, sexy or even better. I'm not really tired but I'm not awake either. I concentrate on following my meal plan and making sure I eat all the meals and snacks on time. I wait, wait for the urge to binge or restrict my food or over-exercise or obsess over food, but the urge does not come.

While watching a TV show, I start thinking about candy, and this is what would happen before. The need would come over me and I'd have to eat a ton of it but my thoughts fade this time. I eat one or two servings of an Almond Joy and I'm over it. My stomach's full. I go to my new day program. It's from 8 a.m. to 2 p.m., Monday through Friday, sort of like high school. I hate the program. Think it's too clinical and impersonal. I say this and get switched to a different program. Still don't like it, but try to make the best out of it. I miss residential. Wasn't ready to leave, and the real world is too depressing. I can barely get out of bed here. In residential I was forced to get out of bed. There is no one to force me here.

For a minute I am excited to go shopping for new clothes but then get worried about spending the money, so now I'm not even enthusiastic to do that. In my eating disorder I'd never let myself buy clothes until my body was right. It had to be a certain weight, the right body fat percentage, correct amount of muscle mass, toned in the right areas and more. It never got "right" so I never bought a thing, and would wear old ratty stuff that was always the wrong size.

Therapists say that after you stop an addiction you can actually feel worse because you have nothing to numb the pain. All the bad feelings that you were constantly distracting yourself from, for example by obsessing over anything and everything, you now have to feel. The loneliness you were trying to soothe and shove down with food, you have to feel too. And the anger you were trying to get rid of with over-exercising, you now have to sit with it.

I do my therapy homework while driving. I'm supposed to think about how I feel five times a day. This is the second time. I feel sad and if I had to be more specific I feel low, like I'm nothing and nobody. But those aren't really feelings, so I feel *inadequate*. I give myself time now, time where I don't have to audition.

I come home from my outpatient program and feel lonely. I know this for sure because I have been taught to identify my feelings. I play with the new kitten that Ashley got even though I didn't want her to get him because I didn't want cat hair everywhere, and any more responsibility. The kitten has very soft fur and allows me to cuddle with him for a few minutes. It's as fulfilling as it's going to get.

I take a short nap with the kitten while watching TV but when I wake up he almost snags my jeans so I push him off my lap. I go to the gym for twenty minutes and don't look in the mirror. I wear a baggy T-shirt but this time it's for healthy reasons. One reason is to not sabotage myself by judging my body. The baggy shirt covers my body so I can avoid being triggered to relapse. If instead I wore a tight tank top I'd see more of myself in the mirror and then might want to restrict because I would think I look huge.

At the post office there is a blond guy. He makes me think of Penn. I want to buy him gifts and mail them to him. I would get him my favorite movies and books I want him to watch and read so we can talk about them. Want to send him cheesy inspiring cards and leather journals with quotes on them but don't. Don't do any of this. I go to Starbucks instead.

At Starbucks I buy iced coffee. Sit out in the sun and read. I make myself do this for two hours a week as it's supposed to be fun. This is my hangout place now instead of the gym. But I can't concentrate on my book. Instead, I remember talking with Penn before we started rehearsal one night.

Earlier in the day Penn did an improv with Jade. The scene topic was marriage. In the improv Penn and Jade were kissing, which turned my stomach to watch. Penn said to Jade, "What kind of sex are we going to have? The kind where we look deeply into each other's eyes, or another kind?"

I didn't know there were different kinds. I looked at him differently.

"What?" he asked. He was sitting on the steps to the stage. He put his cell phone away in his pocket.

"Nothing," I started playing with my hair and regretting the shirt I'd chosen to wear.

"You sure?"

"Yeah, nothing. I was just looking at your pants. They make you look gay." It was a good excuse because he was wearing army green capris, very European.

"These aren't gay."

Rourke says good acting comes across in the way the actor's eyes change; that when they're experiencing something the camera always catches it.

Someone pops a balloon at the restaurant patio next to Starbucks and my head starts to hurt. I close my book.

The kitten is not a kitten anymore. He cannot fill the void in my heart, so when he comes and rubs himself up against my leg, I don't want to pet him. I finished my day program. Now I have therapy three days a week and group therapy once a week, but I feel so depressed and can't remember why I didn't feel depressed for so long. Feel the same as I did before I ever started dieting, before I got an eating disorder. Feel exactly the same as when I was a child.

I have a flashback to a fall evening. I'm eleven years old, lying depressed in my bed after school, in the dark, staring at the ceiling. Hardly anything has changed in ten years. I'm still depressed and don't have the motivation to do anything but lay in bed.

I think about my old addict days or my over-exercising, "purging" days. This is what over-exercising is, when you drop everything, no matter what, to go to the gym. When you're late for work. Late for a funeral, because you were at the gym. When you can't function or think until you've gone. There was a time when my training was to be stronger, with better endurance, and more flexibility, but over the years it became only about burning calories and then about things that don't make any sense from a fitness or even body image stand point; it's just about pushing myself to the max. I wanted to do more, more sets, more reps, more cardio, more time, more days, twice a day, multiple times a day, to the whole day. It's not being an athlete at all. It's exercising without eating, when you've eaten too much or right after a binge, when you haven't slept. It's exercising when you can't sleep, when you're sick from an over-intake of caffeine pills. Stretching in the car at stops lights or while driving, to teach my muscles to stand up straight, to get in a little extra movement, even if it's only stretching. Using hand grippers on breaks at work, every chance I had to burn extra calories. Stretching in bed and feeling the sensation in my muscles while I'm laying down if I'm not able to sleep, to not waste the time and get in more fitness.

Sometimes I didn't think I was fat. In fact I was okay with or liked how I looked in the mirror. Knew I was skinny, toned and had low body fat, but these times where few and far between. Like when I had eaten well or perfectly for a while and had exercised enough to meet my own high standards. In bad times, I'd exercise twice a day and make excuses why I needed to. Such as, it wasn't the right kind or it wasn't enough the first time. Any chance to move more had to be taken. Other times I'd constantly try to burn the calories I ate and constantly be trying to lose weight, body fat and be smaller. If I was absolutely too tired to do weightlifting or run, I'd stretch or walk on the treadmill, anything to get the time in.

I remember people asking if I was okay when I would look sick in the locker room or when I'd sit down at the end of the treadmill with my head in my hands after sprinting, trying to catch my breath. When I would feel really sick from exhausting myself, I would throw up in the bathroom, usually just water because there was nothing in my stomach to throw up, and not on purpose but from over-exercise or in combination with not eating enough. This didn't happen often but it happened the signs were there. I did wonder why I'd get sick, but it never once occurred to me it was from over-training or that I'd run too fast, past what I could endure.

When I was too tired to finish a workout, sometimes I'd go downstairs and buy coffee at the coffee shop and then go back to triceps push-downs. Other times I would leave the gym in the morning after 15 minutes, too tired to do more. I'd promise myself I was going to go back later that day to finish my workout because I always had to finish. There was no giving up and I couldn't live with the feeling of missing a day in my week's routine. Sometimes, I would nap and then go back. I'd stay in my gym clothes until I went back to make sure I'd go. I'd live in a sports bra. They're one of the most uncomfortable things to wear, especially when they're wet.

I trained on holidays, even Thanksgiving and Christmas. By writing down what days I went to the gym and what body parts were worked out, I would be sure it was balanced. Guaranteed I went five or six days a week and spent enough time training because it was tracked. Sometimes I would tally the sets to make sure I wouldn't miss one. Even if I'd finished my planned workout, I'd always do a little extra if possible. It could make me look better, make me more toned.

Bad memories were of riding the escalator to get to my car, feeling so tired and out of it leaving the gym. I'd worry about making the drive home.

Worse memories were of waiting in my car willing myself to get out in the morning. Being devastated by the thought of the grueling hours ahead. When I got out I'd have to do dips and push-ups. I remember waiting in the car and dreading it because I was so drained, but forcing myself to open the door and get out.

My focus and type of strength training and conditioning changed over time. At first it was spending enough time at the gym, then it was having a more advanced bodybuilding program, then it was something else...this went on and on. Toward the end, before I went to residential, my main poison was running. How many miles I could run in a shorter amount of time the better. I was always trying to beat my own time. Every day I tried. This is the opposite of what a marathon runner or athlete would do to improve their endurance. Every run I'd write how far I went and how long it took. Three miles in 26.32 minutes, and if the next day it was up by 7 seconds, my life would seem over. And this was along with a weightlifting routine that would last one and a half to three hours usually, again depending.

In the past I thought exercising was saving me from my weakness with food. There were times I'd eat something really quickly and it would be out of control. At the time I wouldn't know it was emotional eating. Then I'd freak out and roll out my yoga mat and start doing crunches in my room. I would feel the food in my stomach and the crunches would somehow make it better because I was moving and using energy. I had to get the sensation out of my stomach when I felt I'd broken my rules.

I tried to do everything to work out more. For example, by reading books on the elliptical and coming up with ways to constantly burn calories, or by sitting on an unstable exercise ball at work, my personal training job, instead of a regular chair. One time I went out to eat with some people. Afterward, as we were going to go across the parking lot to go to shopping, we discussed whether we should walk or drive. I wanted to walk because that way I could burn calories. I suggested we walk, didn't say it out loud that's *why* I wanted to walk, just that I wanted to. When they didn't agree, the rest of my day was ruined because of my fury with them.

If I did a workout and it wasn't good enough, it would stay on my mind. If I saw someone who was stronger or who could run more than I could, I'd need to do more. If I suspected I wasn't doing back extensions with the right technique, it would haunt me. When I felt worse about my body, I'd usually work out harder. I would notice the back of my legs weren't as low in body fat as the rest of my body and add in more leg curls. I would always tell myself motivating, positive thoughts like "good job" or "you did great today" in my head after each completed set because I thought this was positive reinforcement and would motivate me for the workout. I tried to always be encouraging.

If my feet were hurting and I was exhausted, I'd switch to the spin bike instead of the treadmill so I could sit. I would always vary my routine. When things got stale and were hitting a plateau I'd add something in, like a heart rate monitor. I would judge the quality of a rep by how much my muscles burned and if I felt my muscle fibers twitch.

Though I thought it was bad before, the eating disorder

got worse after I gained 10 pounds and was trying to get back to my old weight and body composition.

Once I was working out late at 24 Hour Fitness. It was almost midnight. The gym was closing and I had to leave but then drove to another location because I knew it stayed open later to keep working out. I thought *I have enough in me to do one more set, to do a few more leg presses*. Other times I'd come home and then do more using the dumbbells in my room. *I have a little more energy and stamina left in me; I can do more and haven't done enough*. This way I can get to my goal body faster.

One time Ashley brought me a cupcake.

"I know you're on one of your crazy diets but I thought you'd love this," she said.

I knew I didn't have to eat it. I planned to just eat a bite but then ate the whole thing. I was so upset with myself for doing that. I was supposed to be trying to lose weight and had already eaten all the calories I was allowed to that day, 250. Plus, I'd already gone to the gym but after I ate it, I changed and drove back. First I looked up on the internet to see how many calories a cupcake has in it; it said 500. The elliptical counts how many calories you burn. So I did it until it said I'd burned exactly 500. It took about 45 minutes. I wanted to get it done as quickly as I could to be able to go home. So I increased the strength level of it to burn the calories faster.

I read an old journal I wrote a year ago when I had my eating disorder to see if it will make me feel better.

*It's 1:30 a.m. I feel tired. I want to take a shower but am too tired. I feel like my skin is disgusting and wished I'd washed my face last night and used my creams because now it looks disgusting. I was humiliated when I saw Beth at the gym because I've gained so much weight and looked horrible and it's impossible for her not to have noticed. People always*

*used to ask me for exercise tips because they knew how
disciplined and knowledgeable I was about exercise. I hate all
my clothes. I hate my hair. I hate my teeth. I miss Penn and
all I want to do is eat candy. I wish I had money and a good
agent and that Penn was here. Then maybe I wouldn't want
to eat all the time. My running time was the best yesterday,
but today I only ran three miles in 22 minutes. Yesterday I did
three miles in 21 minutes and 33 seconds. I don't know what
happened because I thought I was doing good and now it's
ruined. I decided I'll drink tons of diet iced tea to try and keep
me full so that I don't eat. It's my new plan. My jealously is
still here. Sometimes I think it's the worst feeling to feel. I
should probably write what I'm jealous of but it doesn't even
matter because at this point it's everything and everyone.*

> *I stopped journaling to take a bath but only noticed how
fat I was. I looked at my legs. I need to lose weight. I need to
get more serious about it and try harder, and use more
willpower.*

I miss my old life down to the smells, like the smell of
the wood floor that the stage is made out of and the smog
on Santa Monica Boulevard by school. The metallic material
of the chairs at Strasberg. The sound of the bar across the
street after getting out of class at night and hearing people
out on the balcony. I even miss checking my tires to make
sure I parallel parked close enough to the curb, so I
wouldn't get one of the fifty versions of a parking ticket
that the city of West Hollywood has. The city and Strasberg
is where I grew up and now my therapists are telling me I
have to grow up all over again. Maybe I can blame being
left-handed for getting an eating disorder. Sometimes I
think therapy could have helped if I was younger and my
eating disorder had been caught earlier, but now it's just too
late.

In therapy, I learn more about how much of a
perfectionist I was, and that perfectionism has nothing to

do with ambition. It's just the obsessive search for the negative.

"Why do you put so much pressure on yourself?" Rourke would always say to me. He is never wrong. Ever. In the past I knew this about Rourke too, but I would still tell myself that even though Rourke is always right, this is the one exception where he must be wrong. After all, I'm not a perfectionist. I'm just trying to be so great that I have to be hard on myself and highly critical.

I also learn I had a bad childhood. You would think I wouldn't need to learn this, that I should've known, but didn't. I also learn that to survive it I told myself I had a good one and that's why I ended up with an eating disorder.

I feel my feelings now and am not numbed out or distracted from them, but now I just don't feel good enough, or like a nobody, and also terrified and a bunch of other crappy feelings. It's hell and so is group therapy. How is this supposed to be healing? It's unbearable having to listen to other people's stories and the way they talk about themselves. How hard they are on themselves and how messed up their thinking is because of their screwed up families and childhoods. But I'm told repeatedly this gets me in touch with my feelings because otherwise I wouldn't be relating or reacting to what they say and feel, and that once I get my old feelings out, I'll be happy.

I'm friends with all the girls in group therapy. We hang out outside of the outpatient program just to socialize and have fun, or go though the motions at least of having fun if we are really struggling emotionally, or engaging in self-destructive behaviors. Lisa is also in the group. She was my roommate at Sea Breeze and it's such a small world that we are in the *same* step down program. All the other girls from residential live in different cities and states. My first group with Lisa, she said an eating disorder shouldn't be called an *eating disorder*, that it should be called *a knife to your heart*. That was pretty smart.

In group therapy, I'm told I'm so caring and compassionate and my response is I don't know what I say or do to make them think this. I do like the atmosphere of the group therapy room. There is always a lighted candle. We sit in a circle on the floor with pillows and blankets if we want. We all take our shoes off before we enter the room to keep it a sacred space.

I'm in group. A girl just shared and now she is crying and the rest of the group is moving closer to her and helping her feel safe. Two other girls start to cry because they are touched by her story. They can relate and are releasing their own pain.

I'm hating this, struggling to say the least. I feel very defensive, negative and not sad at all. Am questioning the concept of therapy altogether. I'm sensitive, so no matter how many feelings or events I grieve through, more just come. And I've shared my feelings with other people for a year and when I leave group, the depression and anxiety don't lift. Again, Maggie specifically says that when I connect and feel my old feelings of abandonment from when I was a kid my anxiety "fear" and depression "invalidated feelings" will fade. It sounds perfectly right in theory but the problem is I'm practicing it completely and it's not working, so I'm worried this is as good as it gets.

Basically I'm fucked. If I just had acting in my life and some therapy to discuss situations that I don't know how to handle, then I'd be content. Sometimes when therapy is going this bad, I imagine the day I will have to say I'm leaving the group because I'm going to be shooting a movie in France with Scorsese. How else can I bear to listen to this? My future is what drives me and always has.

That's another reason why I miss the smells, because what people, meaning therapists, don't understand is when a kind of person like me has the important things, like being on a movie set and acting, the little things don't matter as much. I'll forget about the smells. The only way to not get upset about little stuff is to know I have or am striving for what I really want 'cause that's what life's about.

I should speak up and say I'm having a hard time relating to the group and feel overwhelmed. I have done this in the past when these same feelings and thoughts surfaced. Thoughts such as, my entire life has been a sham and when I stopped my eating disorder I was hopeful that I was finally understood. That things where going to be okay, and then I just got stabbed in the heart again. I should speak up right now even to say, "I don't know what to say." A stinging pressure is in my chest and there's a lump in my throat. I know as soon as I open my mouth to say anything I will start to bawl because everyone in the room is so miserable except the facilitator, Maggie. But this makes me still not want to say anything because I have spoken up a thousand times in group, and cried just as many, but where has it really gotten me? I still feel so desperate and my life is not at all where I want it. The lump in my throat gets bigger and my breathing shallower because another girl in group starts to cry. I should try harder to somehow surrender to this trapped feeling that's shortening my breath. Then I see Lisa get up and walk out of the room.

What the hell?

For a few minutes I don't know what to do, and then I whisper to Maggie that I'm worried about her. Lisa was not one of the girls who was crying.

"Do you want to go look for her?" Maggie says.

I say yes and leave to look for Lisa. I shut the door quietly behind me to not interrupt the group. I mean, yeah of course I also wanted to get out of the room. Who wants to do this? But I'd never *actually* quit. I'm not gonna choose to be in the gutter again. I'll feel now, even though it hurts. I know her and what she's been through and she thinks she can just walk out.

Does she think she can just give up? If I have to do this,

then Lisa does too. I should try to reel her back in by being compassionate, but I don't know if I'll be able to because I'm mad. I'm going to tell her, "get back in there" when I see her and, "let's go back." And if she is freaking out I'm going to say that the only way not to freak out is to get your freak-out released in group therapy, and that it's either feeling like shit for a little while longer or living your life with your head in the toilet, and that I know it's hard. But I'm not gonna worry about her because I can't watch her throw away her recovery.

Down the hallway I peek in two of the empty rooms but she isn't in either of them. I go down to the parking lot and look for her in her car. I have the urge to take her by the arm and march her back upstairs to the group room. I look everywhere but she's not here. I go back to the group.

# 15. DESPERATE MEASURES

I should be happy I'm already recovered. I haven't had any self-destructive behaviors since leaving Sea Breeze. I eat and exercise normally now and most of my obsessive thoughts about food and exercise are gone. Should be happy I don't have an addiction, but I can't help imagining becoming a drug addict now. I could take the downer, Xanax or become an alcoholic. This way I could get through the day because I'll know when I get home I can have a drink, and then get that warm fuzzy feeling. I think of the ways I can relapse and get what I want and make my future dreams come true, so in case none of this works, I'll have a backup plan.

It's time to do my therapy homework. Again, I feel a little like I'm a kid in school. I write a letter from my body to my mind. The letter is supposed to be my body talking when I had an eating disorder. I get out my journal and lay down on my bed.

*Dear Brain,*

*I wanted to be hugged but you would never allow it. I wanted to rest and you wouldn't allow that either. You kept me awake with a bunch of caffeine. Wanted to wear shorts, skirts and bikinis in the summer and feel the sun on me, but you always kept me covered up. Wanted my waist to have arms wrapped around it, to be able to sleep in, to slouch and I yearned for my face to be touched. To cuddle in a soft blanket more, but you thought that stuff was too frivolous. I wanted to go in the bathtub and feel warm but you didn't make time for silly things like that either. I was hungry and pleaded for you to nourish me more. Let me eat the food that smelled so good. I wished you would've let me stop running when my feet hurt, when my heart was beating so fast that I'd get chest pain. Needed more hugs, kisses and caressing but you never thought those things were important. I hoped for my hair to be stroked and my hands to be held like they do in the movies. I wanted to be able to get messy and dirty by lying in the sand at the beach and walking in the city on a windy day but you never let me play or allowed a hair to be out of place. You always even kept my feet covered up. I wanted my freckles to show but you'd cover them up with makeup. I wanted to be snuggled and tickled and to walk barefoot in the grass. I wanted the window down when we drove. Wanted to jump up and down and dance when I heard good music but I was usually too worn out from your workouts to move. Most of all I wanted to be next to someone, but you always told them to leave. Never asked for much or anything extreme but I hardly got anything, just crumbs. I tried to warn you I was unhappy by having stomach pain and shin pain, but it only made you harder on me. You made me exercise more. You should've listened to my warnings back then. How could you do this to me?*

*From,*

*Body*

I decide to go above and beyond my homework and write a letter from my brain back to my body.

*Dear Body,*

*I'm sorry I didn't treat you well. I didn't know any better. At the time, I just did what I'd been taught. I didn't know you wanted to go out in the sun and play, didn't know you needed to be held tight. Thought only children needed that or you could wait until you were older for romance. I'm sorry I always kept you hidden.*

*From,*
*Brain*

I stop writing in my journal because I can't think of what else to say.

I want to go back to transforming my outer self. I notice wanting to obsess so fucking bad, but when I stop myself I feel crazy. Like, if only I spend long enough cleaning or do it the right way or do something more. Then I'll be able to face my big problems and fears and won't feel disgusting. I want to go back in time so bad it hurts, and there's nothing I can do about it. Back in time, I could redo things and it wouldn't be too late. Or maybe I could go forward in time. I'd do that too if I had magical powers, but now feel as though I've lost my mind. We bulimics sometimes say when we first started to binge and purge, we felt like we were cheating God's punishment, whether it was an over-exercising purge or a vomiting purge. We could have our cake and eat it too. We felt on top of the world for a while and that's why it makes it even harder to live without.

My mind still feels like a prison. I fantasize over and over *what my life could have been like;* make up all these scenarios in my head and don't know how to stop. This is because I'm such an obsessive, creative and detailed person. This helps in acting, but hurts in life. I feel like I can relive, and re-create all of the past in my head, and even feel it all over again. But all I really want to do is erase all of my memories completely, even of Penn and Strasberg, because no in-between is tolerable.

Lisa quits our group therapy. She hasn't been back since she walked out. I've been meaning to email her but haven't yet.

I feel overwhelmed. To fix this I immediately want to clean, get a makeover, facial and color my hair. Organize my room. Whiten my teeth and get a new permanent root lifter, but I don't give in.

I'm bursting at the seams and feel insane. On a walk, seeing a dad teach his kid to ride a bike should move me, transform me and make me feel warm and fuzzy in my body, but all I feel is wanting something external to get better, like having the perfect pair of jeans. I should meditate more, do deep breathing more, journal more and be a better person. I've been screaming at God even though I don't believe in God, which really means I'm desperate and have come to last resorts. Could go running to calm down but that's what I used to do. That was just the eating disorder and running away.

Instead, I plan and visualize everything I could do if I could go back in time. Wouldn't even want to do big things like bet on a football game to win money, since I would already know who was going to win, or play the lottery. I'd want to go back and fix the things I sabotaged and didn't even know it.

Or I dream of going to the future. Envision and plan it all in my head, anything to get out of the now. This is the exact opposite of what I'm taught to do in therapy, which is to live in the now, because this moment is all there is and that's spiritual. But the spiritual thing I choose to believe in is a superficial, tangible piece of clothing. I choose this on purpose as it will never be able to let me down. I dream about the leather jacket I will have when I'm a great success and have so much money I don't know what to do with it. I picked the leather jacket because it's unattached and unconnected. An insignificant object, but has so much meaning, it represents power.

Instead of wanting food, I now get consistent headaches and they aren't even from caffeine. Apparently they're from my blocked feelings, like the acid reflux in my throat. I'm always tired. I vacuum my room to stop my negative thoughts. Back in time is still all I can think about. What am I going to do? There is no medication for this or I'd take it. I should go to Michael's and buy supplies for the vision board I'm supposed to make, or just crawl back under the covers and lock my door.

There is a bad memory attached to every part of my room. It reminds me of the room I grew up in. I remember hiding in my closet as a kid after school. My depressing journals hidden under the bed. My old school work in bins and being told by my teachers and my mom everything I did was wrong. I didn't ever think I was smart and always wanted to run from my own life.

The weather outside is hot, the weather outside is cold; I don't have the right clothes for any weather. I find a new mole on my body. I don't believe for a second that therapy will work but do exactly what my therapists say and commit a hundred percent to my treatment because something tells me my dreams will come true, my future will come true. It will just take time like Method Acting did and it will be better than I can ever expect. Even though most of me was certain at Strasberg I would suck forever, my acting got better than I could ever have imagined.

I do meditation, restorative yoga, take relaxing baths, go on long walks finding myself, and cry and cry over my past with Maggie. Tell all my secrets to Maggie and the group, since they say you're only as sick as your secrets. Feel my feelings and share in group, do the opposite action and don't self-destruct in anyway. Exercise moderately to help anxiety and stress, do affirmations, guided imagery and keep a routine. It's exhausting. Ask for miracles even though I don't believe in anything. If only I could concentrate. I could get through fine if I have a guarantee of a great future, but don't have it. Every day seems the same.

I listen to music, but I'm supposed to listen to my higher power and the music never seems to be loud enough. I shop for things online I could never afford.

I think of an acting example Rourke gave to teach us. He said a line from *On the Waterfront*: "I could've been somebody." Marlon Brando, playing Terry Malloy said it.

*On the Waterfront* was Penn's favorite movie. I wonder what he is doing at this very moment and want to know so bad it hurts. Or maybe he's forgotten me. I watch movies to escape.

Emotions make my nausea and headaches feel unbearable today. No big epiphanies come. I want my life to start changing like in the movies, want to curse my childhood and all the years wasted. No magic fairy tale for me. In therapy, it's just more to face and conquer. I feel like I've conquered it already but where's my trophy?

A weird messy haze descends. Maybe this is what it feels like to come home from war. I know it's extreme, but to another person whose overcome addiction, they wouldn't say it's extreme. They'd agree and understand.

I don't want to pick up the pieces of my life or put it back together anymore. I'm cranky because I'm not allowed to act out, or get relief. I can't drink. Can't do it with food, can't do it by getting a makeover, and can't do it by being a workaholic. So there's nothing driving me anymore.

Before, I had a purpose that got me out of bed in the morning, to service my addiction and obsessions. Had such a purpose I would shoot out of bed to get done as much as humanly possible. Now I don't know what to do with my time, and have a lot of "if onlys."

I go through the five stages of grieving. The first is anger, after realizing when my first destructive behaviors began. I'm mad because I can't do anything to get those eight years back. The second is denial. As if I'm no better off without my eating disorder 'cause I don't feel any better, and it wasn't that bad anyway or that dangerous because I didn't throw up my food and wasn't a severely underweight anorexic. Most of the time I was at a healthy weight so no one could ever tell I had bulimia. The third is bargaining, and most of this gets directed at Maggie. I tell her I'll do anything, if only she will tell me what to do to get better. The fourth is depression, the kind that steals my energy, when the thought of brushing my hair feels like climbing Mount Everest, so I'm incapable of doing it.

Never mind, I only go through four stages of grieving, because the last stage is acceptance and that will never happen because I can't get past depression. I look up acceptance because I don't really understand what the word means, but I find several answers. The one about psychology says it's the act of a person finding the reality of a situation. The Latin meaning behind the word is "to find rest in." The verb "accept" means, "to receive willingly."

If only I had Marissa Cooper's black leather motorcycle boots from *The O.C.* They could mask my damaged pride and soul. The long walks are supposed to solve my problem that I believe is unsolvable, but in therapy I'm taught there isn't a problem I've had that another person hasn't had, and there is always a solution.

My legs and feet don't hurt when I walk anymore. I don't have constants shin splints and my calves never swell. I don't think about how my posture should be. Still, while I walk I want to curse the person or environmental factors that did this to me, because I didn't do anything wrong. In fact, I did most things goddamn right. I cannot find my inner compass that tells me what direction I should head.

I officially lose my mind because I paint my room yellow. The color yellow is supposed to be an antidote for depression and cure me. I don't think drug addicts are losers anymore. I understand it's their abandonment and unmet needs that make them act out. Nothing good can ever come from having an eating disorder. I don't give a fuck what anybody has said. I know for sure because I've looked and looked, and then looked some more.

I want to change my hair. I want to become someone. I want too much and this must be the problem because I don't know what else it can be. I envy people who party, who are out of touch with their feelings and are in denial about how messed up they are, even though I shouldn't. Maybe I should do more or toughen up. I still want my time back.

Nobody sees me as what I am. My mother doesn't understand. I try to tell her, and spell it out for her, but she still doesn't get it.

I want to shine, be big, be alive. The void in my heart is only taken over by obsessive thoughts. Lots of them involve me comparing myself to other girls. My face looks like it has aged. I get put in more therapy because my depression is so bad. As a therapy homework assignment, I start to journal a little bit each day to try and heal my heart. Maggie suggests that, along with writing what comes to me intuitively, I could write positive affirmations and goal-oriented actions I've taken.

*Friday*

*Dear Journal, here is my positive affirmation for the day—I am tough.*

*I think of the Fridays I want to do over.*

*Saturday*

*Dear Journal, the action I took is I read this book Maggie recommended to me about being creative and it made me feel a little less depressed. Also I sat in front of a simulated sun lamp that was supposed to lift my depression since I now refuse to take any more medication.*

*Sunday*

*Dear Journal, I thought about the conversation I had with Maggie about empowering myself and wrote down ideas of what I could do.*

*Rourke says Sunday is the loneliest day of the week.*

*Monday*

*Dear Journal, I took the positive action of going to therapy to get support even though I felt too disgusting to leave the house and be seen.*

*I'm angry at everything down to the glue stick that dried up on me when I was trying to do a craft. The cat meows. I don't know what he has to complain about.*

*Tuesday*

*Dear Journal, I have nothing to say, and even less to write about.*

Maybe I don't need to see into the future or relive the past. I still don't know what to say to Lisa.

Maybe it's time to go back to school and time to go back to work. It's too soon, though, and I still feel I'm not ready to go back to work. At Starbucks I see this young girl kiss her boyfriend and feel jealous. I tell myself the worst part is over, but really, I'd crawl inside the TV if I could.

I'm worried about Lisa. Her eyes look vacant when I see her this week. She's still not in the outpatient program. I don't know what to tell her. It sucks having so many feelings.

I wonder why in my therapy meditation I keep seeing a window, people dancing and laughing inside. I stand looking through the window, always the one on the outside.

I have light moments sometimes and want to hold onto them, these excited energetic feelings in my chest. I want to dance to music, as I wrote in my letter from my body to my brain. I don't have to be drunk to flow with the music. I can be sober to do it. These moments are usually when I watch or hear something really funny or when I listen to a song that speaks to my heart. My imagination goes wild and I'm thrilled. I let the cat sleep on my lap today and it was comforting.

I returned to work at the gym, but not as a personal trainer. I don't want to help other girls lose weight anymore. Instead, I work at the smoothie place inside. It's a bad place to work since I'm recovering from an eating disorder and must deal with food and exercise. I feel like an alcoholic tending bar. Nobody needs salt poured on a wound.

Work makes me feel a little like I'm getting my life back but I still do passive-aggressive things there. This one member is at the gym way too much. She trains twice a day. She has an eating disorder and is underweight. It takes one to know one. I also know she has a problem because of the way she exercises and what she orders from me. I always secretly put an extra scoop of peanut butter in her peanut butter and banana protein smoothie. She needs all the extra fat and nutrients she can get.

Most days I count down the minutes until I can leave work. Why would I want to deal with the times when smoothie slurp lands on my pants? The yuck soaks through to my leg. The harsh lighting and small square footage makes my spot really hot. After leaving I still hear the sounds of eight blenders going off at once, weights banging in the background, and my own voice screaming over all this to yell out someone's drink order. My coworkers don't recognize me without my required visor and apron. I have to wear my hair in a bun. If I just wear a pony tail, it falls and gets caught in the ice chest when I try to scoop the frozen yogurt and fruit.

My boss "cleans" the floor at work with the industrial faucet. She pulls the flexible hose off the sink and aims it at the floor. The result is, I get sprayed with water, and almost slip and fear to fall. She doesn't have the intelligence to realize mops exist and that they were invented thousands of years ago. I'd tell her myself but worry I won't be able to say it without using profanity. I'm trying to not talk back to her and behave as if I'm coming from a defensive place. I tell myself I'll stay together. Nobody knows how I feel on the inside. After all, I'm an actress. I usually put on a damn good show and smile. My secret way of getting back at everyone is by being a fake! It's such a crappy job with horrible working conditions, horrible pay and horrible everything else. I act like I like it, even though I loathe every second. My coworkers don't know I've come straight from therapy where I've cried, freaked out and was seriously depressed. When depressed, I drink coffee for alertness but only one cup, unlike before. For freaking out, I talk to my coworkers to distract myself and ask how they are. For crying, I wear my sunglass until I get to the bathroom and then use the water to fix my running eye makeup, so no one can tell I was sad.

I clean my room. I feel tired even though I've had a good night sleep. I wear more yellow. I think of an email that I'll write to Lisa. What I'll say to Rourke when I see him again. My wanting to go back in time fades more. One of Maggie's journal suggestions is to list things I love, using music, the animal kingdom, *everything*. I feel like this is a weak exercise and don't see how it will heal me but I'm desperate, so try it.

*Monday*

*Dear Journal, things I love: vanilla soy candles, Buffy the Vampire Slayer episodes, ocean water, mist, Lisa's smile, movie scores.*

I start to cry and throw my journal across the room like a maniac. It hits my closet.

*Tuesday*

*Dear Journal, things I don't love but probably would if I was in a better mood: sappy romance novels with hot sex scenes, the sound of certain notes on a piano, Maggie, that baby tiger I saw playing in a glass cage when I was on vacation years ago.*

*It's Veteran's Day or some holiday like that and I'm resentful at the extra traffic I'll have to deal with when I return something at the mall. I think of all the time, energy and emotions I wasted researching the types of organic food, down to the different sub-classes certified by the USDA.*

Instinctively, while watching a dramatic TV show, I prepare how I'll rehearse it if I am acting it and it is my part. First, I'll start to work on relationship and then I'll also think about the little things or details I could do if I didn't have much time, which I probably wouldn't. I'll study the script when I have a few minutes waiting in line somewhere, and follow my scene partner around until I find emotional chemistry from him. How I will make myself stand out with the director so he'll want to work with me again. Are these premonitions of the future or me being crazy?

I am given silk yellow sunflowers as a gift so I decide to display them in my room because they match my yellow walls.

*Wednesday*

*Dear Journal, my list of positive actions: 1. I went to group, 2. I went to work, 3. I didn't lose weight even though I wished I was skinnier, 4. I did almost every assignment in the creativity book I read to help me feel less overwhelmed about my acting career, 5. I wore this tight lace tank top I love even though I thought I looked fat.*

*I have absolutely nothing to write about again except for the fact that my cheap-ass pen is dying and it shouldn't be dying because I just bought it.*

I go to hot yoga today hoping to get a sense of euphoria afterward, the way other people talk about it in group. But the only thing that happens is the mousse from my hair somehow melts on my hands from the extreme heat and I end up sticking to my mat.

Work is taking over my life again, which is not good because it's not the kind of work that leads to anything anyway. It doesn't really pay anything. Basically, it does nothing and forces me to be around loser, deadbeat energy.

I keep going to group. I'm told I'm making progress but I don't feel it or see it. I notice this deep panic I feel at five in the morning when I get up for work. The same feeling in my gut that I've been running away from, distracting from and numbing for fifteen years. This scared ache that is usually low in my gut toward my back. It says something is very wrong and I better fix it immediately and do whatever it takes to get rid of this desperation.

Lisa, who struggles a lot with bingeing and purging, says she wrote a poem to the toilet.

"Can I read it?" I ask her. She says yes and even reads it
to me.

## ~Ode to the Toilet~

*My guilt is dumped out of me.*
*And you ruin my life when I don't want you to.*
*I'm sick of being your slave but I still need you.*
*I need you to flush away my pain, and to flush away the shitty*
*day.*
*To swallow my anger and wash away the misery,*
*to get out my sadness since I don't cry anymore.*
*One day, I decided to stop crying because I didn't want to be sad*
*and unhappy anymore.*
*A decade of tears was enough.*
*But there were tears still inside me so the next day I found you.*
*My tears come out in vomit because this accomplishes something.*
*We accomplish something together.*
*I cried for years in front of my parents,*
*but they said I was overreacting and were never there for me*
*and were mainly the source of my sorrow.*
*So I release my feelings to you as if you're my best friend.*
*I get to vent to you.*
*If I make a terrible mistake I can bow down to you,*
*empty it into you and you'll relieve me of my sin.*
*You're always there for me at the end of the day, no one else.*
*So it's hard for me to leave.*
*When people tell me I should ditch you and we should break up,*
*I worry I'll be alone.*
*Worry that they don't understand I need you.*
*You have done more for me than anyone.*
*Even though I'm starting to hate you because you're so demanding*
*and just want more and more of me.*
*Every time you swallow my shame,*
*more seems to grow inside me and it might catch up to me soon.*
*We did have a lot of good times together.*

*I poured my throw up into you and in return you gave me a clean*
*slate.*
*I'd be pure again and if somebody tarnished me*
*I could throw that up and be pure all over again.*
*But I should abandon you.*
*You make me feel so good,*
*but my best friend shouldn't hurt me,*
*demand perfection and let me hurt myself.*

"It's a beautiful poem… but I think you deserve a greater love than the toilet," I say, and then go on, "Sometimes I feel like that. Miss my old best friend, and it's like this big loss I worry I'll never ever get over."

"It's all I've ever known."

"I know."

I tell Lisa about this poem I read online. It was when a famous actor I admired died of a heroin overdose. I was devastated, all I could think was *but he had everything.* A fan of his wrote the poem in the comments area of an article written about his death.

"I only remember the first line and the last line: *Drugs touch a place that God cannot reach/May you rest in peace,*" I say.

"That's awful."

"Yeah, it is."

I wish Lisa's poetry could save her. If only she writes a lifetime of poems and then reads them to her therapist, maybe she could get better.

# 16. FROM HERE TO ETERNITY

I don't have much contact with Penn anymore. I think about him. He doesn't panic at almost everything like I do, so I worry he doesn't understand me now. What would he say if he knew almost all my energy now is basically focused on fixing my mental and emotional problems?

I'm sobbing in my room while listening to music. I'm bawling over the pain and void in my heart. The twisted anxiety stuck in me and the feeling that something horrific is happening. My raw nose hurts. My phone rings. I see it's Penn but ignore the call. I can't answer hysterical.

I call him the next day and get his voicemail in German. He feels so far away. After playing phone tag we finally catch each other. He tells me how good the movie *Tropic Thunder* is and how I have to see it, but it's an awful comedy about people in a fake war or something. I've seen the preview. It's not the kind of serious soul reaching movie we like.

"The one with Robert Downey Jr., that one?" I ask for the fifth time confirming he wants me to see *that* movie.

"Yes, goddammit."

"Okay. Maybe I'll try to rent it," I say.

"Why are you against laughing? Trust me, you're going to laugh. Though there's a lot more to it than just the humor and it'll lighten you're mood."

"For a second but it won't be enough."

"You haven't even seen it yet," he says.

"Enough talking about me, how are you? How's Ella?"

"She's good. She's in Italy on vacation."

"Why didn't you go?"

"Because she went with her girlfriends," he says casually. It's my way of seeing if they are together and how they're doing. I get my answer they're a couple but nothing about the rest. I assumed they were back together so I don't feel much different hearing it. Penn probably can't tell I'm hinting around even though I want him to. He was right all along. I am naïve for the naïve; don't even know how to hint around. I don't end up watching the movie. It seems so trivial and so does our conversation. Not like how we used to talk, but maybe it's just me and this new broken existence that's so different.

It's Christmas day. Gloomy and cold out, well, West Hollywood cold, and that makes the day even better because it feels like wintertime. Surprisingly, I love the holidays. Especially the biggest holiday, Christmas, because it's the closest day I can have to peace of mind, the closest day to feeling not being in chaos, not having to do anything or be anything. On Christmas the world stops and when I'm just home I don't think of what I need to be doing: cleaning my car, grocery shopping, making a five year plan, working on a monologue, looking up auditions, writing a cover letter to agencies, or researching talent agencies. The list goes on. I can do nothing but not *feel* like I'm bad for doing nothing. It's the day I get to play hooky from myself. My thoughts don't trap me. I can just be. Christmas is the day that society switches its pressure scale, from "you'd better work" to "you'd better not work." In fact, "you'd better be damn merry and relaxed or else." So I'm merry and my mind is not allowed to think or try. It's allowed to be silly and childlike and my day's agenda is to do nothing. This takes so much pressure off me. It's the one day of the year I'm out of the pressure cooker. My energy level even rises on Christmas. For example, I bake cookies today.

I called Lisa to see if she wanted to hang out over the holidays. I don't want to go to any holiday parties or anything similar. In fact, I've been avoiding all those things like the plague. I don't want to be judged for where I am in life and grilled for what I'm doing or get the most dreaded question, "what do you do," because I can't say I'm an actress. I won't be able to talk about the last audition I went on or the part I just got. Because I can't, I'll only feel embarrassed. I don't know what to say to people about where I've been or about the fact that I've disappeared. I don't know what the hell to say and I'm scared shitless people will find me out. I also don't want to go to any parties because I have nothing to wear. I still have no clothes and buying something is way too much work on top of putting myself back together. But I know Lisa will never judge my pathetic life.

Lisa's gonna meet up with her family later, but I don't want to see my mom or anybody later which is okay.

Lisa and I are at my place watching endless episodes of guilty TV like *Gossip Girl* and *Grey's Anatomy* because that's what I want to do. With wet hair, I lay on the couch under a blanket in an old pair of ugly jeans with holes in both knees. Lisa looks cute as always and is dressed for later. I admire her ballet flats.

"I'm craving root beer. Let's go get some after this episode's over. Ralph's is open until one I think," I say.

"Kay, I want to get Mountain Dew. I threw up behind a bush in my backyard last Christmas because my parents were in the kitchen and both bathrooms were being used and I panicked after eating a dried apricot and a candy cane. You know, those kinds that come in those holiday gift baskets."

"Did the bush die?"

"At least I didn't involve anyone else. At residential girls would just throw up at the table," Lisa says.

"Yeah, that happened with one girl when I went. It was weird. I remember feeling compassion for her but the staff seemed pissed. Now I know she could have controlled it."

Lisa's eating a Christmas cookie I baked, one with a Christmas tree design that I made out of frosting. I know she knows it's not about the food. That's good 'cause sometimes that's the hardest thing to learn, that her eating disorder is about her feelings and her past.

"Did you guys have group Wednesday?" she says.

"Yeah, it was small though because a lot of people are out of town for the holiday. You can come back, you know."

"Yeah..." she says.

I notice she's lost weight, which is bad for her because I know she struggles with maintaining her weight. I have the urge to feed her while I'm with her today. Give her the multivitamin I take, and make sure she drinks enough water.

The dark cloud is back. Antidepressants don't work on me. I wonder about other people. I compare myself to them; how they look, how much money they make compared to me, how many boyfriends they've had, how they all seem to be together, normal and feel good. I still don't feel ready to be back at work and am so anxious there. I should be pursuing my acting career but decided to take a break considering everything. I see my Maggie. She's the only other normal person I've ever met in my life, other than Penn, Rourke and the girls from treatment. I tell her how I feel and I want my life to change. She says it takes time. I read self-help books. When I feel my sensitivity, I try to tell myself it makes me a better actress and try to be at peace with it. I feel another headache coming on. I continue to try to change myself on the inside and even though I never over-exercise anymore, I'm still beyond exhausted.

I take walks to find myself. Therapy isn't really helping my body image much because I feel so huge when I walk. It's different now though, because it's not all the time and I know I'm messed up in my head. It's not reality or what other people see at all. They tell me I only feel this way because of my emotional pain.

Sometimes people make comments to me that I caught an eating disorder because I live in L.A. or because it's Southern California. They don't understand. Like how I was never related to and was basically raised by a robot and that can really screw up a living, breathing, human being. My mom never wanted to talk to me, just criticized me, and never taught me that I was extraordinary.

Rourke was the only person in my life who saw me as extraordinary and I was supposed to learn that from a parent. I don't want to believe I'm mediocre.

In group we do a guided meditation, except I see the wrong images. I see epic movie scenes instead of myself. Estella, played by Gwyneth Paltrow, walking, wearing green in central park in *Great Expectations* when she runs into Finn, played by Ethan Hawke. Even my meditation is not right.

I keep going to my horrible job that never gets better. I clean the grit and sour milk off of the bottom of the eight blender motors, and yes, they smell. I listen to my coworker's sad lives. I cringe when I hear a guy at work talk because I'm afraid I'll become him. He talks about his partying days and all the cars he crashed. He has the same low, dead-end smoothie job as I do, a kid that he never sees and another baby on the way, and is in denial because he thinks he's together now. It's awful to hear him talk because I worry his kids will just become alcoholics with eating disorders or develop some other addiction.

In group therapy, my mind can't help but wonder off again. The fantasy of me filming a movie in France with Scorsese grows.

In Paris, the shoot is ending early tonight. The streets here are different. They're paved with rocky cobblestones and I feel good walking on them, like I'm in an exotic place. Steam rises from the gutters. Earlier today, we were running behind on set so there was a lot of pressure on me, but because I was so well trained, it didn't affect my acting or even me. I just thought it was fun.

I miss Rourke. I always imagine him being on set with me in my future because he will always make me a better actress. I've only ever been taught to put the scene first, and how I can improve it, and make it more personal. In acting I always know what to do, or at least know what to try. If the line feels phony, repeat it. If the line isn't motivated, go back to the improv or my preparation. If it isn't personal, speak the inner monologue. Follow my impulses even if I think they're shit. If I'm not sure what to do with a choice, spend more time exploring it. Rourke was there, at least as a guide. His voice is the only one in my head and I ate, slept and breathed acting to get this instinct ingrained into me, and now I realize it is. But the thing is, it's the only thing I've been taught, and although that's needed for the stage and my career, I have absolutely no idea how to live life. I have no voice in my head, not even my own. It's just empty. The inner guidance and self-knowing ways are not here, nor are the answers that are supposed to lie within me. There's no improving or ad-libbing my way to happiness, and that's the first thing in my life I've ever been good at and am proud of. There isn't a director in my head.

I even try to fix myself by writing a list of every good thing Rourke said to me so I can believe in myself. The list goes on and on for pages until it gets so late that I have to go to sleep. But I still have pages to go, and so much more to write.

I remember something so silly about Penn from the past. So why do I care so much and remember so well?

I was sitting next to him in class. We were in the front row. I always liked to be in the front row and it seemed like Penn did too. I leaned over his shoulder to see what notes he wrote down. He turned his notebook toward me so I could see what he wrote more easily. It was something Rourke had just said to the class: *don't trust a choice that, if it works once in rehearsal, it will work on stage. It needs to be practiced and repeated while doing a daily activity.*

Penn didn't get mad at my insecurity, competitiveness and spying habit. He even turned his notebook so I could snoop easier. I already had what Rourke said in my notes, probably several places, so I didn't need to write it down.

Before I met Penn, Matt was doing a play at the ninety-nine-seat theater in school. The cast would rehearse till about 10:30 p.m. and my class got out at 11 p.m. I would always have to pass him when I'd walk outside. He'd be standing outside by the wall smoking a cigarette with a bunch of other slackers. I'd give him a half smile when I'd walk by, and then curse him in my head. He'd usually check me out while taking a break from whatever girl he was currently flirting with. I thought things were bad then. I'd go home and not eat, mostly because I felt sick and would lose my appetite. I would never stay and talk. I always pretended to be very busy. Plus, it's not like we had anything to talk about. He could never go deeper than small talk, which bores me anyway. I did see the play when it opened, and his acting sucked.

"What are you thinking about?" Lisa asks one day, while we sit at The Coffee Bean.

"Times when I was in my eating disorder, but thought I was happy, or at least okay." If someone asked me then, I would have said I was happy.

Whenever I saw Matt I felt like a fool for having had a crush on him. Those were the nights that I always went back to the gym to run. Like Lisa, I wonder what it would sound like if I wrote a poem or letter to the toilet or, well, for me, the treadmill. It would probably be some tale of revenge, written in blood for dramatic effect, or perhaps in over-exercising sweat.

*Saturday*

*Dear Journal, actually, Dear Cybex Treadmill, When I think back to you and of our times together I get a deep twisting in my chest and only remember being in hell. During troubled times I would go to you and run to relieve stress, after already being your slave in the morning. Your cheap media hype, fake fancy labels and glamour made me believe you were a very healthy and smart way to deal with frustration. That sprinting was cathartic and a good way to deal with my sensitivity. You convinced me I was being smart and responsible, because you always said the more miles we go together the stronger person I'll be, and the quicker I'll succeed. You teased me that pounding my feet on you would get my anger out. Get the stinging in my chest to go away, so I'd finally feel free.*

*You stole years from me. I should've been dating boys and going to parties but you always came first so I had to cut everything out to fit you in. I thought I was taking care of myself by being obsessed with you and not partying and rarely drinking. With you under my feet I thought I was being determined and disciplined. That the self-indulgent, wrong thing to do would be to watch a movie or lay on the couch, listen to sad music, feel down and give myself a break. If you hadn't wasted most of my life and made me miss out on so much, I wouldn't be in the place I am now with this awful embarrassing job. I wouldn't be so worried about my acting career that I'll never make it. Or never get one professional part on a TV show. Together we were going to reach new heights. You told me we would win Oscars and travel the world together. I've never been so disappointed.*

*Go to Hell,*
*Blake*

I sit at the coffee shop around the corner from where I see my therapist, Maggie. I just finished a session with her and have a break before group. I brought my journal, saying to myself I am going to do therapy homework on the break but what I really want to do is stare into space and think about my session and where all of this therapy is going. I conclude: nowhere. I've been through too much. If I'd gotten in therapy sooner, maybe it would've worked. I text Lisa to see if she wants to meet me because my thoughts are only making me more depressed.

"I want arms like hers," says Lisa.

I turn my head slightly to see who Lisa is looking at: a woman our age standing in line, wearing a tank top.

"You *have* arms like hers. You're just messed up in the head," I say. I've gotten a good seat, one of the comfortable leather chairs and have an overview of the large interior. "What do you do when you can't get over a guy, and think you're crazy and the only solution you can come up with is taking anti-psychotic meds and deleting your Facebook page so you can't stalk him?" I ask, and then go on. "And when your therapist has you do a meditation, and you're supposed to let what comes up appear in your visual garden. And all you can see is him, and he won't leave your garden?"

"Good question," Lisa says.

"My session went horrible today," I add.

"Did you ask Maggie?"

"We already talked about it but nothing has changed. Maybe I should make a collage or just order an iced coffee. And the group is just gonna say that he was an asshole and that I'll meet someone better. But I want him back so I can make up the past and get a second chance. The way it should've been."

"Maybe this is something you can use in your acting," Lisa says.

"But that's what I used to do and it was never healthy and I just crashed. I can't use everything for acting. And now I know if I have fun and do pleasurable things and not just work and do something to balance me out then overall I'm supposed to feel better and everything is supposed to help each other right?

"Who said that?"

"Maggie," I say.

"Yeah, but sometimes you make up something in your head that isn't true. Sometimes it takes longer then you think to get clear about something or let something go. You have to believe that it's meant to happen this way."

I can't believe I just poured my soul out to her and she thinks she can pull this *everything happens for a reason* bullshit cliché recovery stuff on me and expect I'll buy into it.

"I know this isn't what you want to hear and I should tell you it's insufferable and sucks, that I know how you feel. That you can cry on my shoulder if you want, but well, I think it's good you're longing for him because it means you want people and you're healing. And that before you'd never have admitted it to me but now you're not as scared. Your defensive walls are coming down. Don't think I'm being religious and all new age for saying this," Lisa says.

I hate that she knows me so well that she can predict what I will most likely think. "But how do I turn my mind off and stop my thoughts?"

"Worse comes to worst, distract yourself by watching a lot of guilty TV."

I finally convince Lisa to come back to group even though I am not supposed to get codependent and be a caretaker, but it doesn't seem like she is doing well. I can tell because she smiles too much. Also, because one time before group, she wore a sweatshirt, jeans and sneakers, on one of the hottest, most humid, days of the year. She told me that when she's the sickest, the most anorexic, that's also when she covers up her body the most. Plus, she never shares enough or at all really in group. I always share and participate like I'm told to.

In group with Lisa, I look over to her during a discussion even though I probably shouldn't. I should be getting in touch with how I feel and how I should show up emotionally for myself. Lisa doesn't even look overwhelmed like she used to. She's just zoning out and looks like she might even fall asleep. Why isn't she paying attention? She really needs this. Her eyes are practically glazed over.

Three weeks later Lisa announces to the group that she is going back to residential because she's having so many eating disorder behaviors. The place she's going to is in a different state. It will be the fifth time she's gone to residential. It's a good facility though. I've heard of it and know other girls who have gone and it's got a good reputation. Lisa's been a total mess and didn't even tell me or anyone. Or maybe none of this would have happened.

In group, I say I'm glad she's going because I know she'll be safe there and that everyone needs more support.

That she's just in too much pain and when she has more loving people around her and more help she will be able to win over ED. ED is short for eating disorder.

Then I corner Lisa in the bathroom right after group is over.

"You told me you didn't want to leave your life again," I say.

"I know."

"You said you were gonna try and that you wanted this, wanted recovery this time."

"I did," Lisa says.

"I don't see how anything is gonna change. You're gonna come home and the exact thing is gonna happen again, I know it. The cycle is just going to repeat itself," except I don't say this last part out loud, only in my head.

"Remember when we did that goodbye group at Sea Breeze and it's so awkward and they gave us that necklace that everybody gets and they say we're going to do great and they'll miss us but they hope they'll never see us again because they don't want us to have to come back. Remember? I thought you weren't going to be one of those people. I saved that plastic piece of shit because I did my time. I don't know what my point is. I thought you believed in God and a least you have that and I don't even have that and I can do it so why can't you? I thought you had that higher power, something bigger than yourself in the dark times." I don't say this part either. Just wish I could.

I want to tell her I saved the worry doll she gave me and put it under my pillow even though I don't believe in any of that crap. But I put it under my pillow and used all my therapy skills so I wouldn't worry and would feel empowered. It was when I was so afraid to go on a job interview that my life was practically flashing before my eyes. And then I didn't even get the fucking job and now have to work at this minimum wage job, but have I thrown in the towel?

"What day are you leaving?" I say instead. She misses the toilet. It's her best friend, I guess.

Before she leaves I give her a card and write in it. "I'll miss you. –Blake." I had seen the card in stores before and wanted to get it for her. It's that one with the picture of a tiny kitten staring at himself in the mirror and in the reflection the kitten sees a giant powerful lion with a big mane roaring back. It reads: *What matters most is how you see yourself.*

Penn and I don't talk on the phone anymore, just emails now and then. I tell Maggie about him one session. I have, of course, mentioned him but I tell her more detailed today. "And then he was gone so suddenly," I say. That I didn't realize how I felt about him while we were working together because I was always so focused on school. I tell her about the book he gave me, that it means something to me.

In one of his emails he writes: *It's cool you're back working. Sorry you hate it. I'm sure you can get something better soon.* He sends me a link to his acting website. *I just finished it. It's in German but you'll get the idea.* I look at his pictures. They start to make me sad. Still, I look at all of them. I watch his reel. It makes me miss him and a little enthusiastic, seeing someone I know who gives a shit about acting. There are also links to a YouTube clip and his LinkedIn page, but I've seen enough of his life I'm not really a part of anymore.

# 17. WILD HEARTS CAN'T BE BROKEN

Months go by and Lisa's back from Arizona, where she went to residential and then to the partial hospitalization program as a step-down support system. She calls me to meet up but I don't really want to go and have been still feeling really depressed. I can't believe I ran around the building like an idiot that one time, searching for her when she left group.

I agree to meet Lisa at The Coffee Bean and when I see her I run up to her like a little kid and give her a hug. She has gained weight and looks so beautiful. I am proud of her.

"Are you coming back to group? What therapy things are you taking?" I ask her while we are in line.

"Oh, they got me in a ton of stuff."

We both order. I secretly spy on what she orders, even though I shouldn't. To make sure she's not restricting. But nothing she orders is low fat or sugar free. We head outside to the patio.

"That guy was checking you out," Lisa says.

"Who?"

"When are you going to realize guys check you out all the time?"

"I will, when you realize you're an empowered woman," I say.

We sit under one of the umbrellas with our coffees.

"They were into the root cause of what's wrong and using alternative ways instead–"

"Instead of shoving medication down your throat," I finish.

"Yeah. One of my favorite things we did was a meditation before bed. They put these yoga pillows under the arch of our back and we would get in a restorative pose, I think it's called. Then they would lead us through it. First to get in touch with the sensations in our bodies and with our breath and then it's like we're in this weird place. Almost like we're half asleep and extra relaxed. So our defenses are really low. Then they'd bring in a way to heal. One of the first things they said is 'can you think of someone you want to forgive' and all this stuff popped into my head."

"So who'd you forgive?" I ask.

"I didn't forgive anyone the first night. I wasn't ready. But then it's like eventually, and I know you've heard them say this, eventually you just have to forgive everyone, forgive yourself and forgive God. Not because they deserve it but because you deserve it. To not have to carry all those emotions you don't want."

"But how do you do it? You just think it?"

"Yeah. You just think it. Just decide. What do you do if you think it and it doesn't work? You weren't thinking it in the first place," Lisa says.

"That doesn't make a lot of sense."

"Okay, this is how. You think it, it takes a while, but you

say it in your head and one cell in your body feels better, lighter. And then it grows."

"Well, it's an interesting theory." I drink the last drop of my iced coffee. I take off the lid and suck on the remaining small ice cubes. "I still don't know how you could forgive your family," I say.

"It doesn't mean that what they did was okay. When I got to the real me with the meditation, it makes since, and then almost seems silly to stay so mad or sad. And since you don't believe in God, I thought instead you could forgive an actor who you think is godlike, since you're envious of their big career. It'll be close enough."

I laugh. "Maybe I could."

I start ripping up my napkin in little pieces, making a mess. I tend to do this when I am nervous. I see my Mac lipstick in my open purse I never wear anymore, but still carry around. I read somewhere the wavelengths coming off the color red are supposed to have an attractive effect on people.

I sit in Maggie's office waiting. Mom went to the bathroom and said she'd return in a minute. This is the first sign of her passive aggression, being late. I am having trouble getting comfortable on the couch because my feet hurt so bad from standing at work all day. I notice a drop of green smoothie on my trashed tennis shoes.

Earlier, Maggie said Mom and I should do family therapy because I'm codependent. I'm so reactive to Mom and it's affecting my healing and ability to move forward. This is our fourth appointment. The last three appointments it seemed we were just speaking different languages, and I couldn't get anything across to Mom even with Maggie's help.

The first appointment I spent the whole time straightening out all her lies and it was hard to get a word in with how much she talked. The second session we tried this thing called "when you _____ it makes me feel" and then Mom had to repeat what I said, by summarizing it. She couldn't do it because of her listening problems. "I don't want to do this," she had said. The third session I talked about specific incidences in the past where I felt betrayed. Mom started to respond with how she felt and explained one of her actions but then brought up the time I was late to a family gathering. I yelled at her because I had gotten so much grief for it already. So we never got to anything deep or healing.

Maggie sits on the chair across from me. Mother walks in. We'd fought before the appointment when Mom proclaimed she didn't feel like coming. That she "was done." "I rescheduled twice to make it work with *your* schedule and now you're not coming!" I told her. After, she agreed, but I can tell she doesn't want to be here, done after a lousy three sessions. If I was done after I tried anything only three times, I'd be dead.

Mom's face looks puffy. She seems to be staring at nothing and not really even paying attention. Yeah, her inattention is the story of my life. She is only into her own misery and not able to try because it takes effort. I mean, does she think this is enjoyable for me and like I look forward to it and it isn't uncomfortable as hell? But I will feel uncomfortable for the bigger picture because I'm a grown up, but she's still a child.

"Well, I remember it started when she was at school and had a little part-time job," Mom says.

"But why do you have to call it 'little.' I was working a lot at a hard job, studying all the time, really stressed out and worried how I was going to get everything done," I twist the tassel on my purse.

"I think you should go back on medication. There is this new drug Dr. Armento said—"

Interrupting, I say, "I told you ten times already I'm not going on medication again!"

Mom says, "Dr. Armento said with low doses—"

I cut her off again. "I hate Dr. Armento. If I had my way I'd get his medical license revoked."

This goes on with us arguing, Mom making up stories about my medication history and me correcting her to Maggie.

"I'm not perfect," Mom says.

This is one of her favorite phrases. "Oh, and I bet next you're going to say you're old and that's why you can't remember anything right."

"I'm worried about your depression," Mom says.

She thinks by saying she's worried about me it's going to gain my compassion or something but it does the opposite. It only makes me angry and retract. She always says she worries but never takes action. This is her personality disorder. Saying one thing and doing another. I don't have time for crazy in my life anymore.

"How do you feel?" Maggie asks me.

"I feel hopeless and that she doesn't understand. I don't know how to be any more clear."

"Blake doesn't want to go on medication and since there's a clear disagreement here we should go on to work on something else," Maggie says.

"I wasn't a bad mother. Eating disorders are genetic too, and there are a lot of other factors."

Mom likes to throw in this "genetic factor" every chance she gets to take the responsibility off her.

"I'm angry at you because I wouldn't have had to go through all this and needed the eating disorder if I would've believed in myself. I'm saying there were a lot of times when you weren't there for me."

Normally I'm so angry at her, more angry than I've been at any person in my life but when she, Maggie and I are all sitting in a room and I have to tell her straight to her face how bad I was hurt, it's hard. Suddenly, my anger washes away for a second and a part of me doesn't want to tell her and hurt her feelings. So I say it. But say it while looking at the floor.

"Look at her when you talk to her," Maggie says.

"I don't want to. It's not my personality to confront."

I'm furious at Maggie for picking at hairs or splitting hairs or whatever the saying is. I mean, I'm practically shaking just getting the words out and Maggie can't stop obsessing about this eye contact thing.

"I would call you from my apartment crying and clearly upset. You wouldn't do anything and were never there so I just went to addiction, so that I could be numb."

"You would be so upset over small things like getting a parking ticket," Mom says.

I am ready to walk out the door at this comment because I remember that particular phone call she's referring to. Desperate, but probably not to the point of hysterical, I couldn't find my car and when I did, I had a ticket. It was the year before I went to Strasberg. I was in college.

Actually, I don't remember very much of that time. Earlier, Maggie said I had to disconnect from it to survive it. What I do recall was being on all of Dr. Armento's medication and thought every day if things didn't work out I could always kill myself by overdosing on my meds.

"I was hysterical over everything because deep down I was struggling so much and had no support. It was my way of acting out and asking for help when I would talk about being upset over *little things*. Anyone else would've noticed." I hope to end with a punch.

"Look at her when you talk," Maggie says to me.

"You can look at me," Mom says.

I have a flashback of holding onto the wooden bed post of my twin bed so I won't have to go to school. My legs being pulled on by my mom, so I will get in the car.

And this was in high school. If I would've behaved this way in elementary school, in might have been normal.

"You act like I didn't do anything. I was told I had to let you grow up and be on your own," says Mom.

She deflects again by blaming my high school counselor who I know told her this. Or maybe it was my tutor, but what difference does it make who it was.

"What did you need from your mom when you would reach out to her the year you were away at college?" Maggie asks.

I should be been thinking of an answer but instead I am looking at Mom. She is zoned out and slumping in her chair. Like her muscles are extremely weak.

"I needed help." I wanted to say "and love" but couldn't admit it in front of Mom.

"Lynn. How does that make you feel?" Maggie says.

"My friend, Megan, said her daughter would call her once a year crying and wanting to come home," Mom says.

The reality is I called several times a day in panicked fits.

"How does what Blake said make you *feel*?" Maggie asks again.

"It makes me sad." My mom cries saying this and then stares at the bookshelf. The look in her eyes says she's half asleep and angry. I know she has a lot more to say but won't. She can't take the pain. I regret having dragged her here in the first place. Like the saying goes, a zebra never changes its stripes. Why isn't Maggie commenting on how distant she's being?

"That's it?" I push and twist the tassel around and around on my purse.

"Lynn, breathe; you seem to be holding your breath," Maggie says.

"You used the word abandonment last session and I thought that was a really strong word," Mom says.

There isn't a word strong enough I think.

Mom tells a joke and starts laughing.

"This isn't a time for jokes," I tell her.

"I joke when I feel uncomfortable," she says seriously

and then laughs again.

"So stop," I bark.

Maggie interrupts me. "Let's get back to what Lynn said about the word abandonment, Blake, why don't you explain to her what you meant."

I have a flashback to when I was a kid so I say, "When I was eight years old, I repeatedly said for a month I was scared and didn't want to go to a big New Year's Eve party because I was really shy. The night of the party you told me I had to go so I locked myself in the bathroom. You got mad and sent me to therapy the next week. Making me the crazy one and it my fault. After I went to two sessions, you seemed to forget to take me, and forget you were the one who demanded I go in the first place. Lastly, you pretended the party incident didn't happen at all."

I reach for the tassel on my purse but it falls to the ground. It must have ripped when I didn't notice. I grab the stress ball on the coffee table. I look up to address Mom to answer her abandonment question since I branched off but she's left the room. Not literally, but the look in her eyes is absent. What else is there to say?

At home I explain to Lisa how the therapy session with my mom went.

"So she was, like, 'I did this for you and that for you' and listed them. I just wanted to say, 'do we reside on different planets because you didn't do anything, maybe *one* thing, *one* day and then you forgot about me the other 364 days a year.' And she was getting the timeline wrong and all this stuff. So then we were arguing over the timeline and then I was like 'I just want to get to the deep point.' So anyway, we have another appointment next week," I say.

I sit on the carpet in front of poster boards, magazines, scissors and all the craft stuff that I could muster up, which isn't really anything considering how artistic I am and how much I used to enjoy doing crafts. I can't seem to enjoy anything now. I bought glitter too 'cause it made me momentarily happy and I thought that was maybe what a healed, normal person would buy. Lisa is in the kitchen.

"Are you going to ANAD?" Lisa asks. She is talking about the second group we sometimes go to. It's the acronym for Anorexia Nervosa and Associated Disorders.

"Are you even listening?" I ask. Wondering why I bought gold sparkles and not silver.

"Yes, but you keep talking when I need to stir."

Lisa is trying to teach me to cook so I can save money on groceries but I think this is foolish and refuse to learn, like I don't have enough to deal with already. "So I'm worried I wasn't focused or going deep enough in ANAD, because last week I thought of a joke and just wanted to say it," I say.

"Tell me."

"That's not the point of story. Well, it was kind of funny. Maggie was saying that if we are comparing ourselves to other girls, we need to remember to look at them in their eyes and if you don't know their eye color by the time you were done interacting with them then you weren't looking into their eyes. And through the eyes you connect with another's soul. You're not supposed to really notice their body shape, to stay away from body image and looks. She said this before so maybe that's why my mind wondered 'cause I knew this already. So I was thinking to say, but yeah, if it's a guy, we're allowed to look at his body and objectify him right? We don't have to look him in the eyes?"

Lisa laughs.

I am looking at the stuff I bought for my vision board. The board is made of images which break the censor barrier. The critic in your mind can't function through images. Images reach your true heart, in deeper and more personal ways than through the mind.

In therapy, I have done extensive – beyond extensive, to

the point of obsessive even though I didn't mean to be – research about vision boards and why I should do something so ridiculous and silly. A vision board is a simple collage that's supposed to manifest the ultimate future I want. One is supposed to do grand things, similar to curing cancer. It can attract the energy of the city, land, country and universe toward your goal. Toward what you ask for. Call on the power of the world and planets. Align them to a creative end goal. Able to wake up your heart, pull the force of all the elements, talk to the gods, the creativity creator and spirits. Awaken them to help you on your path.

"Do you want red sauce or white?" Lisa says.

"White. Well, whatever you want."

Now, let's be clear, these... I'll call them concepts, are especially hard for me to grasp because I don't believe in any God, higher powers or anything and never will. But when I talk to Maggie about this she says it can still reinforce my future in my heart. Then I won't sabotage myself. Then I won't give up on myself in big or little ways. Because I've sabotaged everything my entire life without even knowing it, I think I can use all the reinforcement I can get. Plus, there is something in my research that gets to me and sticks with me. I can't exactly pinpoint what it is. Is it the science that is talked about, because science is always a true thing? Or is it the stripping of the fog in a sense? I call it the fog but I'm talking about the rumors that our culture breeds that are toxic to artists. Rumors that say artists are stupid, lazy and are contemplating suicide. That say they can't make a living as artists. When the mind and heart are given a break from these rumors, which I once believed were facts, something so pure and easy is left over. So simple, almost childlike, that it gets forgotten.

The board also apparently makes another concept happen. When you take one step toward your creativity, creativity takes one step toward you. So if you take one baby step it turns into a huge step. On this specific vision board, I am supposed to put images and make a college of my ultimate, true north dream job, which is acting in movies. I am feeling very worried about putting my ultimate dream on this 99-cent poster board as well as feeling completely insane for even thinking about doing this project.

Circling around me is a bunch of torn-out pictures from magazines. The girls from group had given me a bunch of magazines encouraging me to do this sad, manifesting exercise. By sad, I mean this must look like a sad-pathetic-very-desperate-living-on-a-prayer-whimsical thing to do. I try to tear out pictures impulsively and not think or analyze things too much, as this is what my research says to do. A big picture of Central Park sits on the floor in front of me, as well as New York City's skyline at night. Huh, I thought I hate New York. Maybe I don't after all. Maybe I actually like it. I just don't like when people act like the only real actors, or actors who have craft, live in New York and not L.A.

I notice Lisa look through the oven door, checking on the garlic bread. I don't know how she can even see though that thing it is so dirty. I always just open the door. Another picture I have torn out is of Robert De Niro with glasses on. My humiliation is rising. Why have I decided to do this when Lisa is here? I should have done it alone in my room with the lights off.

I hold up De Niro. I want to glue his picture to the poster board because he represents the ultimate actor, or is to me. He has the acting career I want. The acting technique I want, the reputation, the notoriety and ability to create any kind of human moment on screen. Maybe if I just turn off one light in the living room. I hold him up to the poster again and then glance at Lisa in the kitchen. I put De Niro back down on the carpet. I should have done this alone, but the only reason I didn't is because I kept avoiding it and putting it off. I thought I might actually do it with Lisa here, casually before we eat. I pick up and put down six or so ripped-out pictures.

I see a picture with rain. I love the rain. It never rains here. It's Ethan Hawke and Gwyneth Paltrow kissing in the rain in *Great Expectations*. I love that scene; that's why I ripped it out. I wish I had a boyfriend or someone to kiss. I worship that movie. De Niro is in it too. Rourke always used to give examples about his acting technique to teach us.

The scene's primary element is relationship, which is the main element of most scenes. I put tape on the back of the picture and then tape the picture to the center of the white poster board. There is a soft light that makes the faces of the actors glow. They're in partial darkness, but there is enough light to see almost every shadow, like a typical street would be at dinnertime in the fall. The droplets fall sideways a bit, the way rain does sometimes, but it doesn't seem too cold a night for New York City, the big city, where this scene takes place. There's urgency to the kiss and the moment.

"You're making me want to make one too," Lisa says who has just picked up Jack Nicholson. "Where are you going to put the glitter?"

"Nowhere, it's done. You can have the glitter," I say.

"But you just started."

"I know, but it's done. It's supposed to be like this, you know, simple, clear, to the point," I say. I've done enough manifesting for one night. The next thing I know, I am going to be one of those crazy religious people who, let's say for instance, cracks her head open and then prays for it to heal instead of going to the hospital.

"What's the point?" asks Lisa.

"Oh, it's um, getting to create a love story on screen and getting paid for what I'm worth, I think, or it's a pretty picture. Here, if you want to do a collage, you can use these too." I hand Lisa stick-on rhinestones, and a picture of the coastline, since she loves being in nature.

At the table, I lick some garlic butter off my finger. I don't feel any different since completing my project. My board is still lying on the floor. My next step is hanging it up in my room. I can see it from where I sit. Lisa is already done eating and sits on the floor collage-ing up a storm, knee deep in magazine scraps and Mod Podge. I keep sneaking peaks at the picture on my board. How long is it supposed to take to work anyway? That night I use push pins and hang my vision board in my room.

# 18.  A PLACE IN THE SUN

I look at my vision board and think about it. It's still not working.

*Tuesday*

*Dear Journal, I can't go anywhere or leave the house because practically everything on the planet triggers my inner insecurities and pain: malls, the gym, Wal-Mart, even the gas station because they have TVs now. It's not fair that when I'm at the grocery store I have to walk past tabloids and see which "celebrity" has lost or gained three pounds and what the new "it" diet is. It makes me sicker than I already feel. I wish one of the headlines on the cover of the tabloids read, 'What Britney Spears Does in Attempt to Fill the Deep Void in her Heart.' But a headline will never read this because it's the real reason and too deep. People will get bored and tabloid sales will drop. Actually I wish tabloids were banned from the planet.*

*Dear Journal, the new powder I bought at Macy's has a weird overly floral smell so I'm returning it. My two hundred and fifty dollar hair straightener melts and is officially broken. Some things are just too broken to fix. I have a dream Britney Spears is in my group therapy. I wonder if my higher power, the one I am trying so hard to believe in, put her there to give me insight into my life. In the dream, Britney is beating herself up as she talks about the ways she self-destructs with men, cigarettes, food and just about everything she can get her hands on. I cry after I hear her talk because I can't help it. It makes me so sad. And then I wake up.*

The void in my heart now mocks and scolds me and we have become enemies. I cannot possibly deal with it throwing tantrums every two seconds and being so needy. I'm trying to live in the real world for Christ's sake and it wants to take up all my time. I want to rip my vision board off the wall and burn it.

My body does not seem to be cooperating with me and is just rebelling more by making me panic and giving me more headaches and nausea. I do another therapy assignment. I do a hundred therapy assignments. I lay on my bed trying to listen to my inner nudging like I've been taught to do, but instead I just get sad, and then start to fall asleep.

Worst of all that desperate feeling in my gut is still here. That's why I worry therapy isn't working. The only goddamn thing therapy seems to be doing is making me notice it more. Like constantly, even when I'm at work and it's super busy, I still feel it. It hits me at big parties. The moment I'm drifting off to sleep. When I go into a dirty public bathroom stall or drive past a neighborhood with no one outside. When I wake up at 4 a.m. to be at work at 5 a.m. I still feel it, even though I'm slightly unconscious because it's so early. Nothing can trick it or mask it. In fact, sometimes it's strongest then. I have a feeling if the void in my heart was finally filled then the dropping feeling in my gut would go away, and that the two are connected.

I've done everything in my power to fill my heart. I thought if more time went by with group therapy and Maggie and me expressing myself I'd be healed. I'm told the feeling in my gut is from not getting love and my needs not being met. I just don't understand at all and just want the void in my heart to be filled so I can go on with my life.

I listen to music as it's supposed to mend my broken heart and the vibrations soothe me. Sometimes after I listen to certain songs I tell that feeling in my gut I'll be there for it, and that I'm a grown-up now and it's not like before but it can still be terrified. That we're going to go on together. Go to work when it doesn't want to go and be strong when it doesn't want to be strong. I tell my gut it's not going to be alone because it has Maggie and group therapy, and especially I will be there, and the next day and the day after that. However long it takes to be ready to heal and I'll never rush it. I'll just be with it, scared until it's ready to relax a little.

They, I mean everyone in group therapy, says I'm negative and don't realize it. I like epic movies so I don't know how this can be true, movies where the protagonist struggles through fantastic obstacles and overcomes in the end. Like in *Free Willy* when the little boy throws his arm up and Willy jumps over the jetty and is freed and when the men put all the pens on the table in a *Beautiful Mind* with Russell Crowe's character, a time-honored symbol of their ultimate respect. In *Gattaca*, just when Vincent thinks he's caught by the security guard, the guard lets him through and he gets to go on a mission to space, his lifetime dream.

They should've made a movie to scare me from dieting so I wouldn't have gotten an eating disorder. Something like that traumatizing one with Leonardo DiCaprio, *The Basketball Diaries,* which was all about drugs. I remember DARE, AKA Drug Abuse Resistance Education, coming into my class in elementary school and showing me pictures of green rotting flesh, heroin addict's arms who can't even find a good vein to shoot up in. I had nothing to scare me away from dieting.

Sometimes I learn what is under my thoughts. Like a long time ago, hating that girl who talked about eating spaghettiOs may mean I'm scared I'll never get the life I want, and I don't want an empty and unfulfilled life.

I am laying on my bed before I have to go to work. It's Thursday. I'm allowed to be depressed on top of my bed in the day but not under the covers because that would mean I'm not trying, that I'm giving in to the depression. Ashley's cat is scratching at the door but I don't want to let him in as he gets fur everywhere and requires far too much attention. I am too tired to give it to him.

My phone rings. It's probably Ashley calling me from Panda Express or something to see if I want anything, which is nice of her, but I never do because I hate that place. I look at the caller ID. It says restricted. So I answer it.

"Hello," I say.

"Is this Blake?" a male voice says.

"Yes, who is this?"

"It's really Blake?" the voice says.

"Yes, who is this?" I say kind of laughing. This is weird.

"It's Penn."

"Penn Tresch. Oh my God, hi," I say. I'm excited and know I sound excited but feel a pang of sadness and worry my voice may crack in a second. I hope I don't cry. I swallow my tears.

"How are you?" I say.

"I'm on Sunset. I just parked." Penn says.

"You're what?"

Penn said he is in L.A. because of two screen tests he has. He's going to come over and visit me tomorrow. I am happy for him and his auditions but mostly jealous.

What should I wear tomorrow? My clothes are far too conservative and nun like. I'm getting depressed just looking at them. I do have plenty of makeup. I don't know how I'll possibly explain my yellow walls to Penn, but they are sort of a pale yellow so maybe he won't even notice. I need to dust my furniture, but maybe I'll let dusting and some other things like that go.

Maybe I should bring up my Britney Spears dream to Maggie and my group therapy to see if they can decode it, but what do dreams really mean anyway? I heard they're just random nerves firing off in your brain.

I have another dream about Brittany Spears. In the dream we're on stage doing a concert because in the dream I'm a singer too. The stage is black painted wood. Britney and I stand in the middle of it with a band behind us. Bright lights shine on us. Britney's all dressed up ready to perform, but I wear a pair of old jeans and an ugly grey T-shirt that's too big. I feel my shoes on my feet and look down. They're shinny five inch heels, black and gold mixed, and Britney's wearing the exact same pair. The band isn't playing anything. In front of us is a huge audience. I mean a sea of people. More people than I've ever seen, but the stadium is completely silent. You can hear my shoe move an inch on the wood. Thousands of people are moving and dancing and are really hyper but no there's sound, like a TV that's on mute.

Britney turns to me, "See, it's peaceful," she says.

Then I wake up.

I put away a few things in my room, or more like hide

them, so Penn doesn't see them when he comes over. Like my stack of therapy insurance forms. All the magazine scraps of actors and actress, landscapes and other stuff I never used for my vision board. They are all over the floor. I take down a sample picture of a woman's airbrushed face that hangs on my wall. It's the before and after picture, to remind me not to obsess over my completion because those pictures are very fucked with. Maggie gave it to me. It would be completely mortifying to be made public.

The old me, before recovery, would tell Penn to go fuck himself and be bitter and resentful for an extended period of time. The new me tries to make the best of things. Like maybe it would be nice to see him, even for only a visit. He's normal and he's a likable person to spend time with. I might have a good time and want to see him. I won't assume he's calling me out of obligation and because he sucked at keeping in touch, as if it means he's repulsed by me and thinks I'm crazy and didn't care about our scene.

I lock Ashley's cat in her room, which is okay because that's where the litter box is. He meows all the time and I don't want any distractions from Penn and our time together.

I notice my still-disordered thoughts when I wonder if he'll notice I've gained weight. Now I'm at my natural set weight, since I've stopped restricting food. It must be true that therapy isn't working, because I'm so anxious. I'm probably sweating and I feel more disgusting than I've ever felt before. All I seem to be able to think about is how my stomach feels and must look when I sit down.

I am curling my hair. Penn is supposed to be over soon, but I have mixed feelings about seeing him. I have already curled my hair and now I'm touching it up. I run my fingers through the curls. I worry he'll come before my hair has cooled down. Then I hear the door bell ring. I turn and run to the door.

I hug him outside the door. Then we come inside and I hug him again because the other hug wasn't long enough. We hug tight. Then he pulls away and looks at me as if he is... I can't tell, maybe confused?

"Aww," he says. He pulls away from me. "Look at you."

"What? I can't believe you're here," I say.

"I know, it's been a year and a half, almost exactly."

"You look the same." My eyes land on his chest. He wears the same type of shirt he used to.

"So do you."

I was happy to see him, but now I'm mad at him for abandoning me and wish he'd leave.

"Are you hungry? Thirsty?" I ask.

"No, I'm good," Penn says.

"I'm really happy to see you."

Penn and I sit on the couch in the living room looking at pictures on his phone. After each one he drags his finger across the phone to go to the next picture. I scoot over next to him so I can see the pictures better.

"This is the cut I got from this new machine at the gym," he says.

"You take pictures of the weirdest things."

He drags his finger across the screen to bring up the next picture.

"This is the cast from *The Trip Back Down* that ran in October," he says.

Penn goes to the next picture. "This is one of the views from my backpacking trip at Lavaux."

"It looks really high. I'd be scared."

"No, you'd like it, and this is at Ella's birthday in March."

"So you guys are doing good?" I ask like a fool.

"We were but then we broke up."

Ella in the picture isn't as bimbo-like as I remember from the ones I've seen before.

"After we got back together, we were together for eleven months but then the same cycle happened between us and we broke up."

"You mean the same negative cycle?" I ask.

"Yes. So, do you have an agent?"

I hear a faint scratching. It is the cat pawing the inside of Ashley's door.

"Why is the first thing out of your mouth 'do I have an agent?' Why don't you ask me how I am?"

"Your mood is still the same. I missed it. How are you?" Penn says.

"Thank you. I'm okay."

"I'm in therapy. Mostly to figure things since the breakup," Penn says.

"I'm actually in therapy too."

"Is that why you're not in school?"

"No," I say.

"Why not?"

"I don't know...because." Why is he giving me the third degree?

"I haven't been doing that much acting. I've been doing other things, sort of, and I needed to take a break from a lot of things," I say. Should I tell him and confess about my eating disorder and total breakdown as a human being?

I go on, "I'm going to go back to school though. But I'm terrified. I'm going back one more semester 'cause I want to make up for the past and be able to redo it and for it to be regular again, you know." Should I say I asked my therapist what to do to get over him? And how for a long time I wished he'd come back and save me like in the movies. Or that I wished I didn't remember every word he said to me. But now I know that is all stupid.

"Sometimes I wished we'd never met, 'cause then I wouldn't have missed you when you left."

"I missed you too," Penn says. He seems to think for a second. "You were right."

"What do you mean?" I ask.

"You know, about before. I exaggerated that story about the stripper," he laughs a little. I don't think it is funny.

"And I saved that *Hustler* magazine because I knew you'd hate it," he says.

"Good, so you're only like a semi-sick fuck now."

"Yeah, but I had you going for a while, I was good."

"I guess." I think of our improvs when we were rehearsing the scene from *Forgotten Minds* and feel bad. I was really hard on him. Saying things like his girlfriend's fat and he sleeps around too much. What if he hates me?

"I'm sorry. When we rehearsed was I really mean to you?" I ask.

"Don't apologize. I really respect you for what you do, your craft," Penn says this firmly. Like he won't let me get away with it and I shouldn't dare think like that. He is talking about my Method Acting, especially my improvisational skills. It feels good.

I hear feline whining coming from the other room. "Hold on, I have to let the cat out of my roommate's room." I go to Ashley's room and open the door, then rush back to the living room. I sit down right next to him on the couch where I had been before. I put my hand on his knee and shake it a little. I lift my head up to look at him. "I wish you could stay longer."

"I know."

The cat appears from down the small hallway, constantly meowing. "He doesn't shut up. I don't know what's wrong with him. He meows all the time. It's so annoying."

"He just wants attention." Penn begins petting the cat sympathetically. Why is he so focused on the stupid cat? He begins telling me about the most recent play he'd been in and that the director was difficult to work with.

"You have to find a way to motivate it, like we were taught to do. But I know it sucks," I say.

Penn picks up one of the cat's toys, a mini basketball,

and starts squeezing it as if it is a stress ball.

"That's the cat's. It's dirty," I say.

He gives the ball a hard squeeze again, and then ignores me. He continues telling me about the play. He is standing up now, a ball of energy just like I remember. I sit on the couch. "I haven't been in any parts," I say.

"You should be in something."

"I know." Penn is so outgoing. He isn't shy like I am, or a complete mess. How am I ever going to make it? This conversation is not helping my confidence.

"You should send out your reel. That's the fun part. School's the hard part. You get one part and then the person who was in charge of the project will call you for another gig and it starts to work like that." Penn starts throwing the mini basketball in the air and catching it. I just want to grab the ball out of his hand and throw it across the room. What if we never had a connection at all and we were just good actors, and now that we don't have *Forgotten Minds* we will have nothing to talk about or feel?

Penn's story about the play goes on. I can talk about acting for days straight but now I want to talk about other things.

"Then the director said, 'say it sounding untrusting,' so obviously I got pissed," he says and seems to stare at my legs for what seems like the fifth time.

"You can sit down," I say. He must be a little jet-lagged. His jeans have a hole in the knee. He sits down on the couch and I scoot next to him and start playing with the fringe on the hole. "I sent you two text messages a couple weeks ago but you didn't respond to them."

"I never got them," Penn looks at my hand. I am still playing with his fringe.

"Oh." It must have been the international phone lines. "Do you ever get that feeling, no matter what time a day it is that your hard work won't pay off? That feeling the twists your thoughts until you don't know up from down. That feeling only some people feel?" I ask him.

"You should ignore that feeling. Because there is a worse thing. And you don't want the worse thing. When you think life isn't worth living. It's good you get that feeling once in a while. Otherwise, it means you don't even care."

The next night I stand on the patio of Penn's hotel room. Looking down, I see a motorcycle parked on the street.

"Did you rent that?" I ask.

"Yes."

"You should have rented a car. Motorcycles are so dangerous." I say.

"They're not that dangerous."

"You're going to be an organ donor." I argue.

"You don't need to get upset about it. I'm only going to ride it for a week. And, you never had a problem with them before"

"We were rehearsing before." I say.

"I had a dream about you last night. It was like it was a movie. The camera was zoomed in on you walking on pavement at night. You were in, what are they called, dress shoes? Heels? But, it was a scene you were acting in."

"I'm not neurotic anymore. I don't analyze dreams. Did you ever have any other dreams about me?"

"No." He says. But, I see him hesitate and he doesn't cover up his lie very good. And, I don't want to push him. I haven't seen him in so long. Maybe I don't know him anymore. And, even if I try to be positive. Love is blinding. Even genesis actors never had good significant others. A significant other can leave you. A career won't leave you.

Days later we are in my room talking. "Actually, you don't look the same," Penn says.

Oh my God, is he going to tell me he noticed I've gained weight? No, he wouldn't ever say that. But is he thinking it?

"Your hair's different."

"I don't like it straight anymore. Or wavy. Mostly, it's more curly now."

"One thing is different then before."

"It's just hair."

"Did something happen?"

"No. I used to think it looked messy, that's why I would straighten it but it's naturally big and wavy. I don't have any good news to share. I wish it was that easy, like in a romantic comedy or in the movies. That's what would happen."

"No, I'm right. Those old clichés that don't seem to be able to go away, stay because they have some authenticity. Because sometimes they're true; and do you know how else I know? Because Rourke would agree with me too. Or maybe I don't have the whole story yet." Penn says.

His phone rings.

"It's just my brother. I can call 'im back," he says and takes his phone and snaps a picture of me.

"What are you doing?" I ask.

"Nothing."

"I finally know *Forgotten Minds*," I say. "You know how Rourke says the scene is done when the actor knows and understands the scene. There was always one line that I felt I couldn't get right, as personal as the others and something was missing. It's when you as Dustin say 'What are you doing every day without me?' and me as Stacy says 'I've been getting by.' I continue, "I realized the subtext is I've wanted to die because without you I'm alone and everything is so bad. That, in fact, I've not been getting by. Just *say* I've been getting by. The same as I would say I'm tough."

"You know what? Our scene was damn good," Penn says.

214

"It was. I wish I could've known it then instead of being such a perfectionist."

"I tried to tell you but in your mind it was never good enough. I just want to videotape you right now to document this moment so you won't change your mind." Penn says.

"Why haven't you moved here, if you have what's it called, your paper's now?" My obvious way of saying I want him to move back to LA.

"Because I officially got my green card when I was still with Ella. I wasn't going to move then. Unless she came with me."

But, it hurts me too much hearing him talk about her and I find myself changing the subject.

"Sometimes I want to go back to when we were talking and I didn't want to start the scene. Everything was so different then and I was so numb, and you and Rourke were a lot of what I had and, oh, I don't know what my point is," I say.

"I'm glad you told me anyway. You would never tell me things like this even when I tried to get it out of you, and I tried," Penn says.

"I told you everything; or I mean, that's what it felt like. More than I told a lot of people."

He stands up and points to my vision board on the wall. It has one picture on it, a picture from the contemporary movie *Great Expectations*. It is of Gwyneth Paltrow, as the character Estella, and Ethan Hawk, as the character Finn, kissing passionately in the rain.

"That scene was so good," he says.

"I know."

"Okay, you can't tell anyone, okay? I'm only showing this to you. Promise or people are really going to think I'm gay," Penn says.

"Okay, I won't tell. What are you talking about?"

He takes out his wallet from his back pocket. "I put this

picture in my wallet to get me to go on auditions when I don't want to go," Penn says.

It is a screen shot from *Great Expectations*, of Estella and Finn as kids when they first kissed. It was at the fountain in the debauched mansion, Paradiso Perduto, after they first met. I take the picture from Penn's hand and look at it closely. I don't know what to say. I am stunned and there is this lightness in my chest that's never been there before.

I'm so engrossed in the picture it takes me a moment to realize Penn has leaned in close to me.

Penn touches my vision board picture. "You know what? This is going to be us someday, sooner than you think. Or at least it's going to be you who's famous. I forgot to tell you one thing after we finished our scene. I love working with you." He says.

"I love it too."

"I actually had one other dream about you. You know it snows where I live. And, I think I see your head peak out the side of a building. And you're laughing and smiling and I try to catch up to you but the closer I get you disappear. And, then I hear you laughing again and your head is peaking out the side of a different building. You're in a tank top and jeans and you're not even cold even though it's cold enough to snow. I start running towards you but when I get close you disappear again. And, I'm thinking what is she doing in Sweden? She doesn't live here."

"How did the dream end?" I ask.

"It went on and on and I hear you laughing, peaking your head out of a bunch of buildings and I'm exhausted from running and I finally catch up to you. I take your hand and you start crying and saying your cold and you have to get inside. I say 'you're lying, you're not cold.' And, you tell me. 'I was just acting' and 'so were you. You'd never run after me'

'I would' I scream. You disappear again and then peak your head out from behind the side of a gate. Again

216

laughing, and I start running to catch you but my feet are glued to the snow and I can't move them. You stop laughing and all the snow on the ground disappears. A guy walks out from the building and you guys hold hands and start walking away. You look back at me devastated and instead of you disappearing, I disappear. Then I woke up." Penn says.

"After you moved away I thought about you more than I thought I would. When we met, I was in love with this guy named Matt Delsa but it ended up being really negative between us. I never told you about him. I was too traumatized. After what he did to me, I told myself I'd never let a man touch me again." I admit.

"You were secretive. I didn't know what was going on with you half the time. You hid it well. Do you still love that guy, Matt?

"No. And, he never loved me. Do you still love Ella?" I ask.

"Not anymore. After we got back together, I thought I could love her again but I couldn't. And, like I said, we decided to end things. I should go. I have a conference call at 6am because they're on the East Coast."

Should I tell him to stay? But, I don't want to force things. Or, force something that doesn't even exist anymore. I pretty much get his point. He's done chasing me and I blew it a long time ago.

Penn tells me before he leaves what time he thinks he'll be done with his last meeting tomorrow. And, we should meet for dinner after. I agree.

It's Thursday night. Penn asks me about Matt after we order. I tell him the story of how we met and how he first hit on me. That, I should have seen the red flags from the beginning, but I was so naive. We don't end up talking about Matt too much because more enjoyable things come up in the conversation. Penn tells me he hasn't heard back from the screen tests yet but he has a good feeling about one of them. And, I have a silly flashback, déjà vu moment of when Penn and I first met and he was sitting at that white table. When, I wasn't interested in other men because I didn't even want to be alive if I wasn't with Matt. I'd already met my soul mate. And, I look across the booth at who was once a stranger, who sometimes it feels like I've know forever now. He wears a Harley-Davidson T-shirt.

We walk down the hallway towards Penn's hotel room but I start to sink. I know the plan is for him to pack his stuff because he has to be at the airport early tomorrow morning.

He opens the door and puts his hand on my lower back and leads me through the door first.

We're inside. He puts his hand on my cheek and neck and kisses me. I'm slightly surprised because of all the charged times I spent with him where nothing ever happened except us bringing the electricity into the playwright's words. I kiss him back. It's the kind of kiss where one kiss isn't enough and I need more and deeper. My body heats up.

It's three hours later, but it feels like only five minutes have gone by. Now, I'm back to reality and I watch Penn pack his suitcase. I start to help him fold clothes.

"Should I move here? Or, are we going to be long distance?" He says.

"What do you mean *should* you?"

"I mean we have to be long distance until I can afford to move here."

"Then why did you say *should* you?"

"I meant to say *when* should I move here."

"We've been together three hours and we're already fighting." I say.

"We aren't fighting. We're having a discussion."

Penn goes out on the patio and I see him look down at the street. I join him on the patio.

"It looks like I got a ticket. I should go move it. It's a new you." He says, referring to my hair. He touches my hair and gives me a quick kiss. "New nails too." He adds. Then, heads down to the street.

I watch him from the patio as he gets on the motorcycle. But, I don't want to be away from him. So, I grab my coat, leave the hotel room and start heading down to the parking garage.

The elevator opens and I feel the crisp cold of the night. The temperature seems to have immediately dropped. I find him in the corner of the parking garage sitting on the bike. He's looking at the ticket.

"How bad's the damage?" I say. But, he doesn't seem concerned about the ticket. He notices I'm cold and starts buttoning up my coat.

"Darling, I know it's late, but should we go on one short final ride? Or is safety first?" Penn asks.

"One last ride."